Zig-Za

Zig-Zag

Richard Thornley

Cadmus Editions
San Francisco

First published by Jonathan Cape, Ltd., London, 1981
ZIG-ZAG copyright © 1981 and © 1988 by Richard Thornley
Cover illustration copyright © 1988 by Adrienne Judith Sohigian

ACKNOWLEDGEMENTS

Leslie Gardner of Artellus, Ltd., London, for assistance on many fronts. This
book is funded in part by the California Arts Council, A State Agency and
the National Endowment for the Arts, A Federal Agency.

First American Edition

Cadmus Editions
POB 687
Tiburon
California
94920

Thornley, Richard, 1950–
Library of Congress Catalog Card Number: 88-70373
ISBN: 9-932274-45-5

Contents

Gastarbeiter

I WAITED OUTSIDE the main entrance, leaning against the wall and bending round to take the occasional quick reconnaissance through the glass doors. At ten o'clock, the foyer of the Hostel would fill with rowdy, lederhosened youths, barking jokes at each other as they waited to get their Hostel cards stamped.

My time was no longer my own. I was woken at seven; there were small loudspeakers in the dormitories that persevered with a ghastly reality. I hid under the blankets and rode it out, all the orders and the terrible clarion stomp of rousing music which followed.

I didn't make it to breakfast; that was the first misdemeanour of the day. I was an untidiness. Like when I arrived there. I had to have a shower; they wouldn't let me out of the foyer before I had paid to take a shower. I gathered that I was classified as a bacteriological terrorist. Soap: one Mark. Shampoo sachet, State issue: one Mark fifty. Breakfast: seven-thirty to eight o'clock. Blankets to be folded and left at foot of bed. No food to be brought in from the outside. Canteen open from seven to eight in the evening, doors bolted at ten, lights out at ten-thirty. Locker-room open from eight to nine, morning and night.

And here, for the moment, lay the predicament of my polythene bag.

The trouble was that if one left one's luggage one was classified as staying for another night. And if one stayed for more than one night, one became part of the community and thereby entered fully into the spirit of the place; one had to sweep the floors from ten to eleven-thirty. After a week one could wash plates and saucepans. For those slightly less spiritual, the thing to do was to check out with one's luggage each morning and sign on again each evening as if one had just arrived. There was nothing in the book about this. I was enormously entertained by the enraged face of the Hostel Chief each night, while this tracksuited idiot seemed to derive some officially sanctioned pleasure from ordering me into the shower. We managed to get along on a basis of mutual contempt.

But there was no bargaining structure. It was a nuisance when I was, as now, outside the main entrance having forgotten to go to the locker-room to collect the polythene bag. The terms were rigid; it would be an hour's slavery to their broom for one polythene bagful of my necessities.

If I was caught.

I flattened my back against the concrete and inched towards the corner of the wall.

The foyer was filling. There were piles of rucksacks. Jovial young men were limbering up in excitement at the thought of their fifteen-mile holiday trek. These people swept no floors.

A group of five were keeping the Hostel Chief in boisterous flattery. There was a map being spread out on the desk. His advice was being sought. This was a good time to make a move.

I opened the glass door quickly and advanced to hover on the edge of the herd. I camouflaged myself with a stretch and a limber. I tum-tummed a tune in a low voice so as to avoid conversation and bent towards the nearest rucksack in a slight hint of belonging.

'*Pom* pom-pom, *Pom* pom-pom . . . ' some crewcut Adonis picked the rhythm up and banged his walking-boot joyously against the floor. I smiled at him weakly, and moved towards the other end of the room. The

8

Hostel Chief was spellbinding the lads with epic tales of fortitude, fräuleins and leg-muscles. Their happy faces shone with pleasure at this manly talk. There was laughter and back-slapping.

There was a gap of some fifteen feet to the locker-room door. Open ground, no melting into the landscape, no allies. One should lower one's head; one should get lost in meekness. I sauntered tensely across the gap and through the door. I shut the door behind me. I went to the locker and greeted my polythene. Not that it held much, but what it did hold was inviolably mine; a few bits and pieces, a map of Europe, a set of underclothes and a folding umbrella.

A sharp rapping, as of knuckles on wood. Beyond the door the hubbub stopped immediately.

I tip-toed across the locker-room and put an eye to the small glass panel. The young men were being briefed by their Gruppenführer. Already they had bunched into a tight phalanx in the centre of the room and there was now a no-man's-land between them and the locker-room door. They were standing still, arms folded, listening intently. Any slight movement would have been remarkable. I was trapped.

The voice described their day to them. They took notes in small pocketbooks. The voice finished with an inevitable joke, which they supported with their laughter. Then there was a call for some appreciation of the Youth Hostel. It was a brief chant and a stirring hoy. The Hostel Chief acknowledged this and exhorted the young men, banging his fist modestly on the desk. There was laughter as they picked up their rucksacks and marched towards the glass doors; further away from me.

I watched the Gruppenführer shake hands with the Hostel Chief and straighten his green knee-socks, apologising for the slight debris that was scattered here and there over the floor. The Hostel Chief pulled his tracksuit trousers up over his belly and dismissed the inconvenience. I knew why. The outlook was all broom. I walked back across the locker-room and waited to be summoned for the benefit of the community.

There was no reason to feel resentful; it was, of course, perfectly fair that one should do one's bit in gratitude for the system provided. And I had absolutely nothing else to do; I had no plan into which the sweeping wouldn't fit.

There was only a matter of drifting through the city to watch the rich people looking at the shopwindows while the foreign races kept the streets clean. I had no idea why I should withhold my paltry labour; it was very unreasonable. But I would certainly smash a window and climb out rather than concede one brush-stroke.

'So . . .'

The Hostel Chief met my innocent smile.

'Not staying . . .' I shook my head vigorously.

'The time is half-past ten.' The Chief laid heavy and slow stress on the last three words; he repeated them with relish, taking his hand down off the door and tapping his finger on his wristwatch.

'Good.' I decided. 'I'm going to Amsterdam.'

The Chief curled his lip in disgust; yesterday it had been Milan and the day before it was Brussels.

'If you do not sweep today, then you will not stay here tonight.' He was about to pull one of the brooms out of the cupboard.

'Right. Enjoy your sweeping.'

I walked across the foyer towards the street.

I lost patience with watching the consumers and passed most of the day in the tea-gardens, waiting for some impetus to strike. I shared a very strong joint with a glum, silent painter who was so intrigued with the polythene bag that I gave it to him in exchange for another bout of narcosis.

It was beginning to rain when we left the park. I clutched my jacket around me tightly. I shivered and attempted to adjust myself to the world outside my eyes, but it sailed away from me, not to be mediated. There were, perhaps, another two hours of daylight. It wasn't the best of times to be starting for Amsterdam or wherever, but when the painter offered me a room for the night I thanked him and refused.

The painter led the way down some steps into the underground. This bright new transport system was the city's latest acquisition. It made ticket-collectors redundant.

We leapt over the barriers with ease, frowned at by the older passers-by. It was O.K. As long as you were moving and there was purpose, it was O.K. But as we waited on the platform, stranded inside this neon capsule which was held between the silent black hole at each end, there was no correlative for anything human. Instinctively we split apart and guarded our isolation, walking restlessly along the platform, glancing up at the posters and advertisements for cultural events. This airless chamber was a home for no one; you wanted to shout but instead you dug your finger-nails into the palm of your hand so that the pain might challenge the clammy Nothing.

In this lack, we set about desecration; like many others before us. The painter had two felt pens and he drew and scribbled over the posters. Quite clever. Bland clichés. Accusations of sexism. Contorted Hegelian genitives. Slogans. Answers to other felt pens.

'I've just swallowed Baader-Meinhof', said a little voice, trapped unseen between the tight-wrapped thighs of a smiling model. This year's model.

I was compelled to write something up; I couldn't think of anything witty or relevant.

I came to a bare hoarding, where somebody hadn't paid a bill. There was a large, white space; plenty of room.

11

I still couldn't think of anything to write. It posed a problem. I wrote 'This space is reserved for me' in large letters.

I kept my concentration on the putting of the pen back into its cap, and then I stepped away to see what I had done. The letters weren't very large, the whole reservation covered but a quarter of the space.

I couldn't make it bigger because the words were too close together. It was a botched job. It was cautious and not grand or confident. I stood before it, quite frustrated, rather stoned.

I didn't want the space anyway. Let them cover their own blankness with whatever form of deceit they could assemble.

I detected in myself something that was hard and against, and not so lunatic and wayward. I could let it alone.

The train rushed into the station.

I was quickly in the centre of the carriage, before the doors, a collection of bored, vacant faces. I lost the painter. I chose not to sit down. The doors shut quietly. The train started.

I was in a calm, wide-eyed state; standing in the glare of the white-light compartment, watching the sculptures shift in their gallery of seats. Untouched by all this.

The train slowed down and stopped in the tunnel. The carriage lights stammered and shut off, then they sprang back to life again. Everyone was still in their seats. It was black outside. We were somewhere under the city. Bodies remained motionless while individual attitudes built up.

Nothing happened. One small group of passengers hastily constructed a conversation. I was glad that they offered noise of some sort, over and above the rustle of newspapers and the desperate murmurs of the young mother who was trying to contain the honest panic of her child. Other people sat and pretended hard not to listen.

We waited in limbo.

A concealed loudspeaker in the carriage somewhere cleared its throat. Everyone looked up and tried to settle on its direction. Perhaps there were two or three loudspeakers for there was no unanimous regard and the heads looked down again and prepared to receive.

They must have been soothing words that came out; plausible explanations for the breakdown. But it was such a harsh command to relax, it was such an astringent, peremptory balm and it was over so soon, the carriage bursting with void, that the child wailed and I shouted *'Sieg Heil!'* away down the aluminium.

They stayed in silence. I glared at them, immune. The train moved on. We came out of our limbo. I outlasted all of them. Still standing, I watched them get out at each station and I went on to the end of the line.

Late afternoon had blurred quickly into evening by the time I had scrambled over a kilometre of scrubland to the autobahn. The rain hadn't arrived and the traffic purred regularly towards the north. I never gave a second thought to returning to the Youth Hostel for the night. I was well out of the city. It would require as much effort to go back as it would to go on somewhere else. I climbed over the crash barrier, extended my arm and stuck the thumb up aggressively.

It was a simple moral predicament for the drivers, and my own judgment on them was simple. Those who stopped were all right, and those who didn't were cunts. I had hitchhiked a lot; there was no such thing as extenuating circumstances. I had been picked up by people on their way to work, by people in a desperate hurry, by people on holiday, by people going to see their loved ones, by loving couples who wanted to be alone, by women who might have something to fear from rape, by women with children. Some people wanted to talk and some didn't. Some were interested in me, others couldn't

13

care less but were going the same way. The only people who never stopped were priests.

Sometimes it was like testing the state of your karma. None of these people had anything to gain by stopping, and there was nothing you could do to make them stop; looking crippled was no advantage, smiling held no appeal, a clean shirt didn't seem to sway their decision. There was so much surrendered passively to chance or to the abstract or to the mood or the stars or whatever, that any person, wrapped up in aloneness and on offer, couldn't help but feel that the way it went was something of a reflection on himself.

I waited for three and a half hours and no one stopped or even slowed down. Individuals, classes, races, creeds – all passed first under my thumb and then under my curse.

Evening had shunted into night, the grasses had slumped down, I had thrown a stone at every target I could find, I had kicked every tin can off into the darkness and I was still stuck under the sodium lights, my battery of songs exhausted, the road now almost always devoid of traffic.

'Bollocks.'

I wondered what was wrong with myself. Maybe I should have reached out for the broom at the Youth Hostel, been born a month later, accepted the basic tenets of Christianity, bought another packet of cigarettes.

'All right,' I muttered, two hours later, just before one in the morning, 'I'll make you a deal. I'll walk . . . '

I set off, under the clear sky, keeping close to the crash barrier and not bothering to hold out my arm to the dozen vehicles that passed.

The start of a motorway is much the same all over Western Europe. The road was laid directly across the terrain, oblivious to field or forest or village; these were merely picturesque features which kept the drivers

14

entertained and awake. Deserted houses hung in close attendance. Small settlements clung together at a decent remove. Nature hovered in a redundant way behind the crash barriers, there was no sign of life at the side of the road, nothing to summon the walker.

I stuck my hands in my pockets and forced the pace along, the soles of my boots making a peculiarly dull, solid, echoless sound, relieved occasionally by the scraping of the gravel. It was like being inside a building. The sky was invisible, the ceiling was formed by the lines of lights which buzzed energetically. The mass of insects round each one had been attracted by this larger, noisier creature which propped up life, defying the night and bending forward under the strain. The empty road was as if suspended magnetically by the glowing pools of orange; it had no contact with the earth beneath. The road, the lights and the dead space between them – they had a blurred, lazy indistinctness which floated, confusing the senses; an endlessly intangible corridor which had as much to do with the earth as a courtesan's practised murmur of pleasure might have to do with a soiled nappy.

I tramped down this glimmering passage, whose torpor remained constant despite the swift and cursory strokes of its automatic lovers, bent only on their empty release into darkness. I didn't hold out my thumb to them. The glowing embrace of this nocturnal creature made me pause and sit for a moment on the metal barrier. I leaned back against the soft wall I imagined behind me. I might as well sleep. A piece of grass here would not be so much different to a piece of grass ahead, and the night was warm and hazy. This was a home.

It was all right for a while but it was terrible two hours later, with dawn edging under the eyelids and damp sneaking through the clothes; a layer of condensation on the grey metal of the crash barrier above me.

I was up and yawning and tossing the head from side to side in the middle of nowhere with bleakness thrown in. The surroundings were tawdry; I was in that wasteland between the industry of the city and the industry of the farm, land that catered for nothing but idle speculators and mongrel dogs on the run. I regarded it poetically for a minute; one verse was enough before breakfast. I walked briskly on towards the rise of a slip-road, anxious to lose this revelation of realism and the rather tedious complaints coming from the stomach.

I waited now on the slip-road, full of purpose and confident irritation. The only ingredient that was lacking was traffic. There was an entirely static quality adhering to the scenery. I tapped the foot, annoyed. I had no idea of the exact hour but it was certainly time for a few Germans to be up and awake and harnessing their vigilance to the economy.

Ah, good. I heard an engine cough and stir. It had to be a small truck of some sort. I couldn't see it yet because there were trees which cut into my view of the winding slip-road. The diesel settled into life.

'Come on,' I rubbed the numbness away from my face, 'get a bloody move on.'

There was a roar like a convoy of army tanks starting up. I peered with interest, waiting for the first glimpse of whatever it might be. The engine tone dipped and then rose. I caught sight of the juggernaut as it crawled out from amongst the trees, unhurried, flexing itself, uncoiling slowly and straightening as it gained the road. I was petrified with admiration. There were huge letters over the silver body, and a thirty-foot spider's web. 'Tarantula Trucking', I read.

There was only one driver and this character wasn't bothered about rushing into the day. He kept the monster creeping slowly towards the autobahn while he devoted himself to his hairbrush and his long, white-gold hair.

16

The character was in two minds about noticing me. I was so interested that I forgot my thumb. The juggernaut almost stalled to a halt, purely, it seemed, through the noble carelessness of the driver; until the clutch was slammed down and the engine was let off the hook. The cab towered overhead. I waited for the parting of the clouds. The driver's door opened and a face looked down. It considered me much as one might assess a tarnished *objet d'art.*

'Erm . . . *gehen Sie nach* . . . Bonn, Amsterdam, London?' I suggested. 'North? . . . that way?' I pointed.

The face showed no signs of comprehension, or interest. The airbrakes tushed their unwanted pressure.

'Are you from public school?' the face asked, rather casually. So this was the old-boy network.

'Yes,' I drawled, casually.

'Ah, I thought so.' The character retracted his body and head and lifted a cardboard box off the mate's seat to place it behind him on the lower bunk-bed. He gave a slight toe to the accelerator. It was taken for granted that I would climb in. I did.

'Good. Well. Breakfast and a wash-up?'

We shook hands and introduced ourselves. The airbrakes came off; Jade put a little reggae on the tape deck and we drifted down towards the autobahn as I settled into my comfortably sprung seat.

Jade didn't say anything, occasionally he would tap his signet ring on the rim of the steering-wheel in time to the music. I had a hard time keeping awake.

'I should sleep. I'll get you up for breakfast.'

I nodded my gratitude and slipped away into a blankness punctuated by sudden, violent half-dreams which jolted me back momentarily. And then as I looked out at the empty road sliding beneath us, my head slumped sideways and I dozed again.

The airbrakes drew me back, several rushes of pressure and a left arm edging the short gear-lever down a couple of notches, the engine whining high at the disruption. We pulled over to the exit lane; I stretched as we glided up into the service area, Jade juggling the gears and the brakes until we slunk to a halt between two other juggernauts. The engine was revved and left to die.

'What time is it?' I asked.

'Quarter-past seven.' He checked his watch carefully. 'We'll take an hour.' He sat and looked through his time-sheet, calculating how long he had driven and how far. He was well into the day, I was struggling far behind him.

'I never was much good at maths. They change it all back at the office so it looks good. You just have to hope that any inquisitive policemen are as incompetent as I am at adding up. A day and a half from Italy. You have to be breaking some kind of regulation to do that.'

'Then what?' I showed a drowsy interest.

'Either a warning, or I lose my licence.'

'What's the hurry?'

'If I didn't break the law, the company would use someone who did.'

'Do they pay you for it?'

'Of course.'

'A lot?'

'Yes. If I make a mistake then I get killed. They don't make roads for truckers, not so that you can drive safely and keep the boss happy. Maybe that's why the wages are good. Hours cost everybody a lot of money.' He scribbled his way through the time-sheet, throwing the clipboard on to the bunk behind him. 'It doesn't make any sense to me. As long as we get out of Germany, we're O.K.; anyone else will take a few quid and stamp anything. If you get out first I'll lock the cab.'

I opened the door and slid down the eight-foot drop to the ground. I banged the door shut and stood yawning.

The other trucks were curtained, the drivers sleeping even though a motor on our own rig was still shaking noisily.

Jade slammed his door and walked round the front of the cab.

'Coming? It's a bit cold for standing around.'

'What about the other engine?' I asked.

'It's the motor for the fridge. This is a cold-store trailer. Twenty tons of apples.'

'Where to?'

'I don't know yet. We have to telephone from Ostend to find out. That's the way the boss works. Once he's got them back, they go to whoever offers the best spot price. Economics is a bit much before breakfast.' Jade smiled.

'Are you going to leave the freezer motor running?'

'Yes.' Jade meandered elegantly across the truck park with a briefcase hanging from one arm.

'Won't it wake the other drivers?'

'Too bad. Rotten apples aren't worth any money. They're what's paying. Once, when the fridge unit packed up, I drove through from Innsbruck to Frankfurt to get a mechanic. If one apple goes off, the others rot in sympathy. They load in an hour, fridge to fridge. The housewife thinks they're fresh, but they're all last year's crop. There's no such thing as a fresh apple, frozen apples make more money. When you're talking like that, who the hell cares whether some foreigner gets another half-hour's sleep . . . '

I looked back across the park and already, in the truck we had pulled up beside, a fat, vested figure was swinging himself down from his bunk. He scowled at us. I followed Jade through the glass swing-doors of the restaurant.

It didn't appeal to me, the motorway service-station; with its slippery food, its restless, function-ridden occupants and its grating Muzak. It was a fitting monument to its customers' disdain, an accumulation of horror guaranteed to render an interlude as irritating and therefore as short as possible. It was rarely beneficial to consider, or even regard, what you ate. It would have been more apt if vitamin and protein pills were issued from automatic dispensers next to the ship-torpedo games and the star battles in the foyer.

'Not a bad place,' Jade approved.

'Yes . . . ' I tagged on.

We went to the washroom. I gingerly smeared a little water over my face. Jade stripped off his shirt, plugged in an electric razor, shaved himself carefully, put the razor back in the briefcase, ran a basinful of hot water, washed face, ears and neck, flannelled down the top half of his body, put on a clean shirt and brushed his hair into shape. I washed my hands again.

With the same methodical application, Jade walked up and down the line of food, picking out a cold orange juice, three slices of toast, butter, two cups of coffee and a Perrier water. He ordered a ham omelette. He glanced over at my cheese roll.

'*Zwei Omeletten*,' he ordered; the server turned to the hotplate. 'No one goes anywhere on a cheese roll, not driving a rig like mine.'

'I'm not driving,' I said, feeling for what money I had in my pocket.

'Why not?' Jade scrutinised me. 'It's only forty foot, ten gears, thirty-something tons. You can drive a car, can't you?' He smiled.

'Yes.'

'All you've got is something that's a bit longer; and if you crash it you're going to do a lot more damage to whatever you hit than you are to yourself. You don't have to worry about cars. They get out of the way all right.'

'Yes . . . ' I enjoyed the laugh. Jade paid for the omelettes, and the way in which he sat down at a Formica table gave the restaurant an aura of the Juan-les-Pins beachfront. He munched slowly, finishing everything on the tray.

'You get inside that cab and you're the king. The others are just small-time artists.' He sat back and burped quietly into his hand. 'They shouldn't be allowed on the motorways, they just get in the way. If there were no cars on the road we wouldn't get tied up in accidents. There's no way you can cause an accident unless you're drunk or you fall asleep or you're useless, and then you shouldn't be on the road anyway. Most car drivers are useless.'

'Have you got a spare shirt?' I asked.

'Back in the cab. We'll do some arranging. It's a small living area. People get on my nerves. I don't usually stop for hitchhikers; they clutter up my space.'

'Unless they're from public school,' I jibed. Jade looked at me.

'I went to public school. I'm proud of it. I enjoyed it too. Like I enjoy doing this. If I didn't enjoy it, I wouldn't do it.'

'And the money's good.'

'When I left school I went through a hundred thousand pounds in a year and a half; yachts, parties, California, women, the lot. I enjoyed spending it. It got a bit boring towards the end. Some people spin it out into a lifestyle without doing anything else. The day I get fed up with motorway food, I'll quit. What've you done since you left school?'

'University.'

'Any good?'

'It was a convenient way of spending three years doing nothing much, I suppose.'

'Doesn't it get to be a habit?' Jade reacted with a shiver. 'Why not?'

'Too much philosophy. I can never think anyway. I'm going to have another coffee.'

21

'I'll get them.'

I returned our trays of debris and fetched the two cups of coffee back to the table. Jade was leaning forward, half asleep.

'What's the plan then?' I pushed the cup across into his fingers.

'Thanks. It's . . . Wednesday morning. I want to get to Ostend as early as possible, pick up the night boat and get to London for tomorrow lunch. I'm a day early and I get Friday off. I've got a girl in London.'

'I thought you might go on to Dublin.'

'No, he won't send me that far. He'll send one of the others. We'll drop in London. I've been north a couple of times on the run, he'll try to find someone else. If I go to Dublin, I get there late Saturday night and I get turned round again Monday morning.' Jade raised an eyebrow.

'That's a bit much, isn't it?'

'It *is* a bit much, it is. It's pushing things a bit. It's right to push drivers, that's where the money is. But then they can die on you. I keep telling him that.' He sipped the coffee and laughed. 'He doesn't believe it. There was an older guy called Mike, who went off the edge of a viaduct in France. Three hundred feet. It goes almost straight down, the trailer on top of the tractor. There's no chance you find anything much. They didn't bother to look for the time-charts. It was the booze. The office said and we agreed. I had *one* glass of wine with him outside Rome. It wasn't the booze. From the time I saw him until the time he died, he had an average speed of forty-five. He must have gone straight through. I wouldn't do it, but . . . there are times. So . . . home on Thursday?' Jade pushed back his chair. I calculated.

'That's continuous driving, isn't it?'

'Yes . . . no . . . not really. Anyway, there's two of us.' There were two sides to be taken for granted.

'We'll see'; I didn't.

22

'We're both from public school, faceless, inter-changeable, no chin. You can do it. I'm going to switch the motor off and get some sleep. Wake me in half an hour.'

Best to do it quickly, this getting back; the most part of a thousand kilometres would be over with by midnight; no extraordinary distance but something of a rip through time and space all the same. I had once driven a Volkswagen van, the juggernaut was only a bit longer and a bit heavier, ten gears, airbrakes, and not that easy to stop. As long as we were going straight, there wouldn't be much call for a tight three-point turn, no traffic lights or roundabouts. Twenty-something tons moving at seventy miles an hour, call it a hundred kilometres an hour, two and a half thousand kilometre-tons impetus; mass, speed, metal, gore – I considered it, the stomach was jack-knifing round on the head, omelette skidding. As long as nothing got in the way, like a party of school-children on a zebra-crossing. Ten, fifteen years in jail?

The Muzak piped merrily in the background. Not much could be worse than that. With a bit of luck I might manage to hit a Muzak delivery van – apples crush Muzak – or I could reverse peacefully through the plate-glass window and over the multi-coloured carpet –apples crush Wurst and Kartoffelsalat Empire. I glanced up and saw that it was at last day proper.

I went to sit on the grass verge, watching the multi-national juggernauts arrive for breakfast at their diesel-hole, edging round each other warily. The tyres on the trailers slid like tank tracks as they were pulled up into line.

I had nothing to worry about, it would be a miracle if I managed to get Tarantula out of the parking-lot, tushing on the brakes, looking into three mirrors at the same time, spinning the tractor from side to side like a worried sheep forced to the front of a thoughtless, hounded flock.

It was the size. The monstrous enormity of the unwieldy mass and the concentration of power at its head. It was, after all, only a matter of lugging weight, there was no independent brain or motor down its back, it was merely a head and a girder with wheels, not unlike a trolley. There was only the tractor to drive, unless the trailer skidded and took on a mutinous life of its own. Then you more or less gave up, I supposed, as I played with a piece of string and a block of wood which smacked into the oil-stained kerbstone at my feet. I winced.

It would be a fine day, anyway; it looked as if it would be. There was no sign of any rain. The sky was teetering between dawn grey and light blue, the voices of the birds persisted through the joking of the truckers, the idling engines and the sporadic bursts of noise from vehicles on the autobahn behind them. It was a placid moment. I relished it.

It was eight-thirty and time to wake Jade. I strolled to the toilets, gave the face a wipe and drank down some water to clear the aftermath of the coffee. When I emerged, Tarantula was already murmuring and I saw Jade balanced on the trailer. I walked quickly across the park, placidity behind me somewhere.

'All right?'

'Yes . . . ' Jade dropped to the ground and peeled off his rubber gloves. 'Watch the grease, keep it out of the cab. We'll fill all the tanks here and that should take us out of Germany.'

I swung up into the cab. I chose the passenger's seat. The top bunk was clear except for a T-shirt and a pillow. Jade hoisted himself into the driver's seat, revved the engine and gave a few perfunctory strokes at his hair. He stretched his eyes wide open and shook his head.

'The start of Wednesday the eighteenth,' he said.

'We've already done a bit, before breakfast,' I reminded him.

24

'Seventy kilos. That's a bonus. That's just waking up. Now watch. Ten gears in two sets of five, high and low ratio. Here's where you switch over and start again. You'll use all ten. If we were empty, you could get away with starting in fifth; but for now you'll have to work your way right through them. Don't rush it; there's no such thing as a fast get-away. It takes a lot of power just to start moving.'

It was more of a tap-dance between brake and clutch as he manoeuvred the truck out of our parking space. The weight behind us was in sudden conflict with the tractor. There were eight gear-changes and much wheel-spinning before we could roll at walking pace over to the pumps.

We lost twenty minutes in waiting to fill up. Jade became angry and impatient long before we had finished. He treated the tractor savagely, bucking it away from the pumps and cutting up a line of cars to get out on to the autobahn. I looked down at the worried drivers and laughed.

Jade went through the gears as fast as he could; we picked up to fifty-five, sixty miles an hour and he sat back with the wind howling past us.

'That's it; from now it's on automatic. The only thing to watch out for is other drivers. If they get in your way then you close up behind them and scare them until they pull over. When you overtake, remember that you've got forty feet until you can pull in. On a three-lane stretch you never take the fast lane, the police are very tight and anxious to be seen doing their duty. They hate you and so does the general public. What do you think?'

'It seems all right.'

'It isn't very difficult. If you're on a mountain pass then it ages you a bit – trying to stop her running away – but there's nothing to worry about on this road. It's just a matter of cruising. It's more comfortable being the driver than the passenger. You'll enjoy yourself.'

'When do you want me to take over?'

'I'll go up to Karlsruhe.'

I lit a cigarette and passed one over to Jade. He gazed out of the window. We overtook a labouring Italian. I smiled condescendingly at the driver, who was admiring our progress.

'It goes well.'

'She's the best; one of the best. I threatened to quit unless I kept this cab. It gets you down driving a bad rig when you've got five hundred miles to do and people keep passing you. You want to be the fastest on the road. You can see the punks in the rigids pretending they're big, and then their mouths drop open.'

I laughed at Jade's obvious pleasure.

'And girls, you get a lot of girls. Too many. Beautiful girls. Classy. I don't do it much. Sometimes it's a hassle. They all want to run away from home. When I finish driving, I like to go to bed.' Jade talked mostly to the mirror.

'Yes . . . ' I yawned.

'Get some sleep. There's nothing happening. It's a good time to sleep. I'll take us on.'

'It's not being antisocial?'

Jade snorted. 'I was never any good at cocktail parties; and I'm so used to being alone now that I can never think of anything to say to anyone. It's always either "excuse me" or "get out of the way".'

'Wake me if you want anything.'

'I will.'

I finished my cigarette and flicked the stub out into the morning. I climbed over the seat and lay along the top bunk. The engine wasn't quiet but it was steady and lulling; there was a pleasing touch from the air that poured in through the slightly opened window. There was a sign over the dashboard: 'Old Truckers never die, they just keep moving on'. Jade seemed to have already

26

forgotten my presence; he was engrossed in the road. I saw him reach for a tape and I heard some of the music during my sleep.

I awoke feeling hot and restless. We were moving fast; the scenery hadn't changed that much, the music had been turned down a few decibels. Jade was absorbed in the autobahn. I put myself back into a doze, until I felt the intrusion of irregularity.

I opened my eyes. Jade was shifting from gear to gear, his shirt hanging open, the cab bouncing uncomfortably. We were stumbling along slowly, hampered by a mass of traffic. Jade muttered and swore.

'Where are we?' I asked.

'Outside Karlsruhe,' Jade growled. He wasn't anxious to unwind; there was an intensely claustrophobic mood in the cab, a pent-up violence which he guarded to himself.

'Anything I can do?'

'You can change the tape.' Jade jerked his head towards the box of cassettes.

'What do you want on?'

'Anything.'

'Irish country music? Early French meditational hymns?' I suggested. 'Or Second World War marching music?'

Jade laughed. He settled back in his seat and stopped tapping his signet ring on the steering-wheel.

'How are we doing for time?'

'It's eleven-forty.' Jade didn't consult his watch.

'That's all right; two-fifty kilometres to Karlsruhe, another two-fifty to Cologne; we're O.K. What's the hold-up?'

'It looks like an accident. No sweat.' Jade grinned. 'This rig just isn't built for stop-start driving. It's ... er ... '

'Sacrilegious.'

'Probably. It's a pain in the arse and a lot of work.'

27

'If you let a bit of a gap open up and take a run at them, we should be able to smash our way through.'

'Mm . . . '

Jade tickled the accelerator and we moved forward, closing the space between us and a sand-coloured family Volkswagen in front. We reached fourth gear, our line of traffic was making progress; but the family man chose to bide his time. Jade kept rolling. I paused with the cassette. Two children waved from the back window, Jade ignored them and their eyes slowly opened in excitement. They put their arms round their granny, she began to turn her head and then they were so close and low down that they were lost to sight, somewhere underneath the cab window. Jade kept rolling. I glanced at him; he sighed disgustedly and slammed his feet down on the clutch and airbrake simultaneously. We stopped dead; so suddenly that I thought we had hit the car.

Just as we stopped, the V.W. pulled neatly out from underneath. It accelerated quickly, covering the fifty open yards, and it halted again behind the steadily moving file of traffic. The granny commented crossly; she wound herself round to glare back at us, the children laughed. Jade went back to square one, jerking us forward, his left arm tensed and his foot pumping.

'Inconsiderate arsehole,' he summarised in a resigned fashion.

'How much space did you have left?'

'Three inches. Some people just bait you. They resent the size. They were brought up small. Small people. You're big and they hate you. They can't be bothered with their gardens but they all want fresh food at their local shop the whole year round, even if there's six inches of snow on the road. They should ban cars from the autobahn, stop them wasting our time and our fuel.'

We came up to the crash and both of us made a point of ignoring it. In the cars around us, people craned sideways to lap up the disaster. There was plenty of room to pass by, the bottleneck was only caused by spectators.

'Sickos.' Jade blasted the airhorns loudly. A policeman looked over and Jade gesticulated helplessly at the inquisitive faces. The policeman nodded and whistled the traffic through. Jade signalled his gratitude. We left it behind.

'What about lunch? You hungry?'

'Not really,' I asserted, after the flesh and tangled metal. 'Do you want a rest?'

'No, we'll get on to Cologne. I wouldn't mind if you did up some cheese and biscuits from the box, and there's some orange juice to wash it down.'

'It seems daft to stop now.'

'I'm not in the mood for it. We'll pull over for a coffee in an hour and a half. Let's kill another hundred kilometres.'

I assembled the cheese and biscuits, then put my feet up on the windscreen ledge and just mused. The road was good for that, endless miles flowed underneath and it was hard to stop a thought following them. Jade said very little, changing the tapes when they ended without choosing any particular music or tempo. The passing towns were only names, a series of *Ausgang* boards on the side of the road. We kept the Rhine away on our left; Heidelberg might have been beautiful but we skirted it.

'You never feel tempted to leave the motorway?' I remarked at the end of a train of thought.

'Sometimes to sleep; otherwise only to drop or pick up. It's not worth the hassle. I suppose that you could cut corners and save on distance, but once I'm on the motorway I stick with it. It drags you along, keeps you moving; otherwise there's a lot of beautiful places. You'd stop. Here, you're in one channel, marked Home. It's good news after a week or ten days.'

'Where's home?'

'Sometimes London, sometimes Dublin. A couple of nights. And you?' Jade demanded.

'I don't know. I've lived in the same place for too long, I'm sick of it.'

'I know what you mean. I was even married for a while – eighteen months. That was enough. We ended up talking about curtains and television programmes. And then there were dinner parties. Sorry darling, I can't make it; I'm in Milan. Thank God.'

'Did you get divorced?'

'Yes, she's gone back to being my girlfriend. She comes out on the road sometimes; we get on a lot better. I stay at her flat in London, I've got a room in Dublin. That's about as much home as I want, outside of this rig.'

Frankfurt.

'How was Munich?' Jade broke the silence this time.

'I didn't stay there long.' I tried to remember. 'Much the same as anywhere else.'

'I get that feeling about Germany. Trying to be like America, but they don't realise that the only interesting thing about America is the people. Sometimes.' Jade lit a cigarette.

'I was in France a year ago; a farm up in the mountains. About a dozen of us.'

'Communal?'

'Yes.'

'I couldn't stand that.'

'Couldn't stand what?'

'Living with a lot of other people, sharing everything.'

'It gives you a chance though. There's not much you can do on your own except get a job, earn a wage and then spend it on leisure or save it for the big dream which gets further and further away and a bit of a sad wank in the mist of your own routine.' I stopped, surprised at my own vehemence. Jade squeezed a length of cigarette ash out of the window. 'I found it a creative place. There isn't very much of that in England.' I ended, embarrassed.

'You can still earn good money in England,' Jade considered.

'You can,' I back-pedalled.

'There's too many people who can't be bothered to do it, people who don't want to take any challenge,' Jade grumbled.

I shifted my feet. Jade looked in the mirror and moved down a couple of gears to be ready to pull out and overtake a cocoon of hippies in a camping bus. I expected him to cast some scathing remark, but what little scorn he had he directed towards himself.

'I sound just like my bloody father talking to me when I refused to work for him.'

'I think it's just that other people's challenges don't interest me for some reason. A pay cheque is such an unconvincing victory. I should basically be plotting the overthrow of the State, but I can't be bothered with the challenge.'

I picked my way through the bewilderment. Jade laughed. 'Let me know when you start. It sounds like fun.'

Wiesbaden.

The sunlight started to fall back in on itself and acquire a dull density, it wasn't a day that would hang on to us. Jade removed his sunglasses and straightened his back.

'Not quite,' he blinked. He claimed the sunglasses again from the dashboard and shook them open, sliding them close up to his eyes.

'What about this coffee?' I suggested.

'You want a break?' Jade asked.

'Don't you?'

'Not really.' Jade hunched over the wheel. For some time now, we hadn't bothered with music. I wondered if my presence was annoying Jade.

Limburg, Ransbach; Jade was still leaning apathetically on the wheel. There was very little traffic, we were cruising at a fast, steady speed.

'End of the harvest,' I commented on the passing countryside. The words sank into irrelevance. I felt as if I was wooing a moody and unwilling lover. I felt nervous and noticed our speed.

We were waging an impersonal war on distance. Not out of hatred – for Jade was in a kind of stupor – but from a remorseless desire to annihilate.

He was frozen and bland; his whole attention absorbed by the surface of the autobahn, he fixed on our destination indifferently. We thundered on; it wasn't a good time to interject, nothing much could have reached him. Even our fellow travellers seemed to respect the intensity. The slower vehicles hugged the side of the road, one or two speed merchants flaunted their privilege to the fast lane. There didn't seem to be any casual drifters about. It must have been the time of day for the professionals. It was a human mood, surviving the glare of the midday sun and now tempted out by the feeling that twilight was not far off.

The central lane stretched open in front of us and Jade never needed to move out of it. The pattern of the traffic was so static that it was as if we were all embalmed on some gigantic conveyor belt of the posturing dead. Passengers and their drivers were preserved in a variety of boxed scenarios like actors pulled up at a dress rehearsal by their director. I watched.

Once again, I found that thoughts were shifting ghosts, anxious to be gone from any brightly lit interrogation and disappearing away behind me; as likely to be recaptured as *that* patch of flowers or *that* clump of couch-grass which swayed on the side of the autobahn as we passed, and then sprang back free and flustered in our wake. There was no preserving of impressions and images and memories. They were flung up out of the air like insects, bursting open to a brilliant, flaring death on the windscreen. Picking them up to reconstruct them was a waste of time to anyone but the most obscene taxidermist.

We were coming off the road, I realised; as if in a dream I was entranced and powerless. We were in the nearside lane, the truck was dipping over on to the hard shoulder. We were bumping. The grass was close and distinct even as it rushed by in its thousands of blades held against the falling sun.

'That's it for me . . . ' Jade exclaimed. 'I'm too exhausted. We'll wait for the rush hour to finish in Cologne. Then you can drive her yourself.'

He slammed down gears and brakes; I evicted my daydreams and stepped down into the late afternoon civilisation of the Cologne *Rastplatz*.

It was the big halt. Perhaps a hundred and fifty juggernauts were pulled up and silent, waiting for the minion commuters ahead of them to disperse.

It was like walking through a fairground. There were splashes of colour and nationality, oil and the throb of motors. Some drivers were alert and joking, others weaklegged from tiredness and the sudden weight of their bodies. Jade took time to brush his hair before walking across to the café. He stumbled once and his right shoulder twitched involuntarily from fatigue. His eyes were cloudy and vacant.

We went into the café and he had friends. I collected coffees and joined him at an English table; he was sitting mutely before an argument about routes which was abandoned as soon as I put the cups on the table. Introductions were made: Irish Johnny, wiry and covered in oil; Tom, thickset, bearded, smiling eyes; his wife,

Mary-Ann; John, who was in on the argument with Clive and Charlie – they moved round to give me space to bring up a chair.

'Well . . . ', Tom summarised, 'there's no saying which is the best way round it. If you're happy with your route, then it's the one for you.' They all agreed. Tom stirred his tea.

'But that pass is a bugger for my money, apologies to you Mary-Ann for saying it. I remember that spring . . . '

There followed a quarter of an hour of the wildest story-telling I could recall; failed brakes, skids, Christmas Eves, blow-outs, nudges, shunts, deaths, laughter. It was all a great performance; I noticed Jade smiling; he was at home.

'Bit of a shock seeing you.' Tom scrutinised Jade. 'The gaffer had you down to leave the day after us.'

'Good time and a quick pick-up.' Jade tapped his saucer with a teaspoon.

'You watch how you go.'

'I do.'

There was a moment's silence, which Tom stretched out paternally.

'We all push it a bit when we want to,' Charlie interrupted Tom's worry. 'There's not one of us that doesn't. If you're young you can take more of it.'

'You *think* you can take it,' Tom cautioned. 'Are you pulled in for the night?'

'I'm not driving any further,' Jade shook his head.

'Well now that's a piece of luck,' Johnny perked up out of a plate of ham and chips, 'otherwise the gaffer'll go thinking we've been lying around on the Italian beach again . . . ' The stories resurged, taller than ever.

'How's Beth?' Mary-Ann asked Jade, underneath the chatter.

'She's well. She's just starting a new job.'

'Give her our love.'

'I will. She mightn't be doing much travelling any more.' Jade made it look as though it was the first time he had considered the possibility.

'Sure that's a weight off your back.' Johnny was irrepressible; Jade smiled. 'Jesus did you ever see the woman that feller Les used to bring with him? I swear to God now, that truck had three speeds and the slowest among them was when she was in it. I'm not kidding you. Every night he was the man for making her sleep in the trailer; she wouldn't sleep in your bottom bunk and he was terrified she might fall down on him from above and knock the life out of his body. He was more scared of that woman than he was of a shunt when she was loaded. Terrible state of affairs for a man to be in. She was that big he would get her to hold up the side of the tractor when he changed a tyre.'

Slowly and inevitably, they regaled Jade back from his fatigue with the help of another coffee. He was still something of an outsider, not only because of his age and lesser experience. It was strange to them that someone with his background should choose to work the rigs. To them it was a sign of stupidity or ill-starred luck; they treated him kindly and slightly wondering.

But most of the stories were directed at me, to entertain me. They themselves must have heard the same tales over and over again. A naive listener was a delicacy; most of the men were taxed by the loneliness they took so much pride in.

'That'll be about it.' Tom looked at his watch. 'The car folk will all be back at home. We'll be going through to Aachen before we sleep. Nice and gentle.'

Mary-Ann came back from her wash and he stood up to leave.

'What are you doing, Johnny?' Jade asked, when they had gone.

'I'll be going through. If your road from Liège is as

dead as it might be. I'm thinking on six or seven hours to the boat from here; I've not been doing very much today.'

'Will you tell them we'll be in too, for the freight boat.'

'That'll be the four of us. Charlie will rest up tonight, John will travel with myself and the feller Clive there wants to get home.' Johnny didn't bother Jade with advice about tiredness and danger. 'We'll have a few beers together.'

'I'll be forty minutes behind you.'

'You eat your food in peace. Not wishing any rudeness,' Johnny bowed to me, 'but he has the better engine than all of us.'

'Who's doing Dublin?' Jade queried.

'I'm going on to Manchester. If I was you, Jade, I'd be letting the others think you're staying out tonight, and I'll ring up the gaffer from Ostend and tell him Clive and John are home. You don't want to be worrying yourself with Dublin. That man would have you going half-way to the moon as a favour to himself; you're much too easy on him.'

I watched Clive and John thread their way back from the toilets, through the crowded tables. The English were in a minority and were by far the quietest. The room boiled with relaxation.

'Keep the gangplank down,' Jade smiled.

'I will; you'll be on that boat or I'll kill the captain myself. Sleep well, boys.'

'See you sometime.' John arrived and shook hands quickly.

'You'll get a good night's rest,' Charlie played at being envious.

'I will,' Jade nodded. 'Safe home.'

'Safe home.'

They went out.

'Let's get some food; there's not enough time for a

36

shower. Too much talking.'

'Good stories,' I assured him.

'Oh yes, they always are. I don't know where they get the energy.'

Jade ordered from the waitress. It was a different standard of food from the autobahn restaurant; it was good food. I had looked around ravenously while they had talked, and had pointed out to Jade what I wanted. It didn't disappoint him.

'Have a wine,' Jade suggested.

'You're the one who's resting, I'm going to drive.'

'I didn't say get drunk; you could have the one glass to take the panic out of it.'

'Who's panicking?' I demanded.

'You should be. It's not a piece of cake. They tell these stories fairly flippantly but most of them are real enough. I sometimes get nightmares about glancing in the mirror and seeing that trailer swing out to pass me.'

'What happens then?' I poised with a fork in mid-air, ready to devour instructions.

'Pray. That you don't get whiplashed.'

'All right, all right . . . ' I shut off imagination. 'You'll be staying awake.'

'I'll be on the bunk behind you. If you get stopped by the police, we change quickly. If we can't manage it, you will have to be me; I'll leave the papers out. Glass of wine?'

'O.K.'

My stomach was right off its food, but I forced it to accept. The food seemed to hover without rising again. Having made his point, Jade lingered over his meal lovingly. I was on the spot with my nerves.

'This one's a good café,' I bid for less silence.

'Yes, it's a truckers' café. They treat truckers well on the Continent. The Dutch have private clubs for truckers and freight agents. Good telephones, telex receivers, message boards. Decent service. And it's always clean.'

'Not like England,' I deduced. Jade was alert with anger.

'England's a shit pit. Some French drivers won't touch the food. You can't park a rig outside a middle-class restaurant. They bring their own food. It's pathetic in England, I find it embarrassing. I pretend to be Dutch. And it shows in English drivers. Most of them sit down covered in grease, no change of clothes. Good drivers; it's not their fault; the chair's probably an inch thick in sludge. The English have got no idea how to treat drivers, the society is too slow and brainless. If a guy earns a hundred and twenty, a hundred and fifty clear per week and works hard for it, he doesn't expect to sit down at a filthy, sticky table with a plate of greasy slop in a place where he can't find a towel and soap. People who work have got no status in England. It was a shock to realise that. And truckers have got no status at all. Pushed out of the way into some back room somewhere. You get a lot of respect over here if you're a long-distance driver; you get what you deserve. The English are snobbish and stupid. I'm not proud to be English.'

'A hundred and fifty quid a week? Clear?'

'Yes.' Jade paused. 'About that.'

'What about tax?'

'The official wage is only forty a week, everything else gets put under expenses. I'm not going to get taxed. Why should I? I'm only in the country three days a fortnight. England does nothing for me, it never paid for my education, it doesn't pay for my health. I bank it all in Germany. At least you get the feeling that you mean something. Working in England is like slavery. Most of your money disappears and in return you get a lousy pension and a rotten health service. You're one of the few people I've met who's got an intelligent attitude to England. It's pointless working. Where we're different is that you prefer to stay and do nothing, while I prefer to get out of the place and get rewarded for what I do. There's no difference really, except that I'm irritated by wasting my time. The money's good, but it's not a question of money; I don't get much time to spend it and there's no point in me spending it on anything that doesn't fit into the cab. But I'm not going to give it to the Government or the State, whatever you call it politically, because the only time they take an interest in me they just bloody interfere with my job. And I'm the one who's responsible for that truck, bringing those apples back. If some bloke in a ministry wants to do something for me, he should open a café where they serve decent coffee, not blather about my hours. I don't need a nurse, I'm in no hurry to commit suicide. He could make good money out of serving me scrambled egg, instead of me paying him to tell me what to do from behind a desk. Even my boss doesn't do that.'

Jade stopped, noticed himself and smiled.

'Well, do you want to go?' He tapped his cigarette packet on the table.

'Yes,' I said.

'Let's get on with it. I don't get paid for arguing about the working class. Not like some of the people I was at school with.'

It was dusk. Jade leant forward and switched the head-lights on. I rubbed my hands against my thighs to get the sweat off them. We had run through the gears already, without the engine. It required some strange muscle at the back of the arm between the elbow and the shoulder – the gear-stick was small but didn't move easily.

'Let's just go very slowly out of the park. You've got a clear run, there's nothing in the way. Feel how the engine reacts and you'll notice the tug from the trailer. Keep the tractor moving slowly and then you won't jump. It feels like you've still got the brakes on, but you haven't. Have you?'

'No.' I checked.

'Airbrakes. Air. O.K.'

I switched the engine on. I heard the air pump in the background as the engine settled. There were several sounds. There must be more controls than I knew about. No. There was only one set of controls and I knew them all. It was going to be straightforward. I looked out at the dusk, the violet hues were deepening, a shrub might have been made out of velvet in the half-light. I put my hands on the wheel.

'Right. Slowly.'

A B.M.W. flashed its lights and sped past us, accelerating fast. I tensed. I had still to be reminded that there was anything else around us.

'Don't worry about him. Ignore him. Right. Clutch. Gear. Pull it harder.' Jade lunged forward, exasperated at my weakness, and pulled us into gear. 'Be hard with it, it isn't going to break.'

'It's an unusual muscle,' I snapped.

'You'll get used to it. Sorry. I'll leave you to it. Build up the revs. Not too high. Don't rush it; we won't get above third until we're out on the road. Take it slowly.'

God, I thought, we haven't even moved yet. Just let us bloody well move. I felt the jerk as the trailer woke up to what was going on.

'More revs.'

The cab seemed to rise up in the air as the trailer hung on stubbornly.

'Move dammit!' I prayed, sweat collecting under my arms.

'You're letting the revs fall,' Jade said sharply. 'Keep them up or you'll stall her.'

'Fuck off!' I slammed my foot down. We moved suddenly, a great dragging weight.

'Change. Now!' Jade helped immediately with the gear-stick. We engaged again. 'Wait. Now change!' I did. 'That's the fast changes. You've got more time. Don't worry about him. Screw him!' The car went past, I felt sick as I realised we'd covered several yards without me once looking out of the windscreen to see where we were going.

'What's wrong?' Jade demanded.

'Where?' I flailed mentally.

'Unless we go faster it's going to take us an hour to get out of the park. Don't forget your mirrors.'

Mirrors, windscreen, mirrors, windscreen, mirrors – that was us, that shadowy silver length.

'Turn slightly, line her up, more revs. Change!'

I managed it on my own.

'Bring her round, haul it right round. Now back again. Anything coming in from the left?'

'No.' I peered in the mirror, the lights were well back.

'Right, get out there and straighten up. Watch the kerb on the left behind you.'

We were too slow in pulling out. There was a car on the slip-road, coming up on us. I would never pivot the trailer out of the way in time. I went for the brake.

'Don't stop!' Jade shouted.

'It's his right of way!' I shouted back, but accelerated all the same. I pulled the trailer out and turned it, cutting off the lights that were now behind us.

'He must have slowed down,' I explained to Jade.

'Of course he did. He's not going to challenge you. You could roll over him without noticing it. People are going to treat you very politely. It's your road.'

'Good.' I kept the tractor pulling.

'Change! Look at the revs.'

Another change; and we trundled. I had a moment to consider where we were heading. We had reached twelve miles an hour. The weight was with me. I had executed

the change smoothly and felt for the first time that I had a
foot in the door. At least I knew the cab. Now I could
concentrate on the road and plan.

'Let this guy get past.'

What guy? But he was already going past on the
passenger's side.

'Now you're clear. Take her up as high as you can and
then see how the brakes feel.'

I did as I was told. The brakes were good.

'You'll have to come down a gear.' I did, with effort.

'O. K., you've got fifty yards until we hit the motorway.'

It was difficult to believe that we had crawled only a
hundred yards in all that time. 'Let's get up into fifth
again, quickly; then cruise and watch your mirrors for
pulling out. You've always got the extra lane if you can't
do it – that goes on for another hundred yards. But do it
as soon as you can. Don't pull out if there's another truck
in the mirror. Cars can get out of the way easier.' We
rolled towards this next test.

'What do you think?' I asked.

'About what?'

'Whether it's a good idea.' I felt weak and drained.

'You can drive her; I can always tell by the end of the
park. You can drive her unless you don't think you can.
It's up to you.'

'O. K.' I kept my eyes on the road and took several deep
breaths to steady myself.

'But remember that you're going out into civilisation.
Don't do anything sudden. Do it smoothly, so everyone
can see.'

We came to the end of the slip-road. I dropped back on
the speed so that I wouldn't be faced with the need for a
gear-change while I was switching lanes. I lined us up and
concentrated across on the mirrors. The autobahn seemed
to be spotted with headlights. I picked out the nearside
lane and kept my eye on it.

'Just crawl. Take it easy. What's behind you?'
'I think it's a truck.'
'Let it go.'
It was almost on us and it thundered past not seven feet away from my left shoulder. I didn't blink.
'What now?'
'Two cars, close; then there's a gap. How much extra lane is there left?'
'Plenty.'
I waited for the cars to come up and buzz past us. The car behind flashed its indicator and moved across into the central lane. Others followed suit. I had never received such kindness.
Do it.
I spun the wheel and the tractor was out on the autobahn.
'Not so sharply. Keep her as straight as possible. That's right. And don't forget you've got gears.'
We were out there. We had our own lane and it went on indefinitely. I had a knot in my throat. Jade's incitement to change gear didn't impinge on me; I managed it without fuss. I felt as if I were running a temperature. I relaxed slightly. 'I forgot the indicators . . . ' I almost laughed.
'Not to worry, we're well lit up. Now let's get moving; work slowly up the gears, listen to the engine.'
I got to seven and mastered the ratio switch before the next experiment.
'I'm going to have to overtake,' I complained, as if it were unnatural.
'There are worse things in life,' Jade teased wryly from behind. 'Same thing again,' Jade recited. 'Watch your mirror, give yourself plenty of time to pull out and straighten up, no angles. Get in the centre lane and stay there unless you lose a lot of speed. You don't want to be in the position of worrying about people; let them

overtake you as a rule, they can use the fast lane. If you have to pull in, just remember you've got forty feet behind you. We don't want to knock some bloke off the road with the trailer.'

It was thirty kilometres before I allowed myself the luxury of pulling in; this time, I made the centre lane and stayed there.

'That's fine,' Jade said; I heard him lie back along the bunk. 'O.K., you've got a clear road. Take her up to top and cruise at about sixty. No rush. When we hit the Cologne ring-road, drop back to fifty and keep an eye open for drinkers and cowboys.'

'Right, chief.' I took the programme. I felt Jade's smile.

I worked us up to sixty-five and dropped back to sixty, guarding the central lane. There were few crises now. The traffic kept away from me.

I felt in control, I slowly adjusted myself to become aware of the shadowy cab. I altered the position of the long-distance mirror. I felt the sweat pouring down my sides and back, I was awash with it, it made me realise my nervousness again. I tested the brakes lightly, I tested the acceleration and the indicators, dipped and undipped the headlights before it finally became dark and I would need them. All from this perch, high up over the road.

I was in the centre lane. Things ahead were moving at my speed. I was pulling a large weight to England. It was normal. We hadn't crashed. I knew how to control it. The unexpected would stay out on the fringes. It wasn't beyond me.

'Sorry about the anger there, Jade. I was a bit nervous when we started off.' I proposed a smile. My lips twitched. I stretched them into confidence; a relaxed smile, for myself. 'I'm enjoying it now.'

There was no answer. I lined the rig up so that I was sure of the next two hundred yards, then I risked a quick turn of the head. Jade had his mouth open as he slept. I turned back quickly and wiped the palms of my hands on my jeans, one at a time. For long minutes I felt utterly powerless over the mass and the speed, as if I was being drawn along by it, uncontrollably; as if it wasn't paying any attention to me at all. I dared not touch it, for fear that this would make no difference to our mad rush. My hands wandered between gear-lever and steering-wheel, my legs seemed to be unreachable. This vast weight was all behind me, propelling me of its own accord. I was in a small cabin, swept away at the front of an avalanche. I was falling. It was the seduction of vertigo. My mind moved too fast for my limbs to react; the speed was in command.

I reined myself in. It hadn't been ten seconds. I could tell that by the van travelling just ahead of me to my right, which I was going to pass, quite comfortably. The force wasn't destructive. The pace of my mind synchronised gradually with my body. My hands were wringing wet, so I dried them. I wondered if I should go on. I decided to give it another five kilometres. I remembered another thing Tom had said at the café, stirring his tea. Either you control it, or it controls you; and once it controls you, you're finished.

I could, and would, control. A second nature.

'Cologne, Aachen, Liège, Brussels . . . ' Jade murmured.

'You're awake . . . ' I felt cheated.

'No. She's yours. Look after her.' Jade turned over and he did go to sleep.

I wound up the window. It was getting cold. I watched the dusk fading, and the headlights stood out more clearly. I no longer saw any shapes, they all hid behind the lights; red and orange and white, small marker lights. With the window closed, a silence swamped the cab. It was very detached, even from the noise of the engine. I kept my eyes on the road, my eyes were out there on their own, ahead of me. I understood why Jade rarely spoke; it intruded on the clearway of impressions and messages

between the eyes and the body. It would be like talking
during a film in which you were always a split second
ahead of the actors. You couldn't tell them what was
going to happen because they were out of reach. There
was no point in entering into conversation with one of the
audience. The very act of talking grated on the eyes. It
ruined your involvement with the show. And I was
captivated by the show. In a car you can express or
compensate for your moods; cars are instruments. In a
juggernaut, you can't compensate for anything. You can
perfect yourself as an instrument, put yourself on automatic and cruise. I appreciated this, the matter of control
evening up into two balanced horizons; I was no less of a
machine than it, in the world of machinery.

There were other things to appreciate. The Cologne
ring-road. The soupy haze of the sodium lights, the
broad sweep of the autobahn as it curved round the
town, the brute echo of engine noise bouncing back off
the crash barriers. The view away down the length of the
trailer surprised me – the pools of light scurrying over its
vast silver surface before dropping back into the road.
Small wonder that meadows and trees fell by the wayside.

I started working us down through the gears, following
the speed limits impeccably. I swung us off to the right
and down a wide bend which curved back underneath
the ring-road and then straightened out into the Aachen
autobahn. Back up through the gears; traffic joined us
from the right, each car judged its entrance around my
progress, briefly forming a respectful convoy for the
truck until it sorted itself out to pass or to fall back. And
then we were free from Cologne; the lights were few and
far between, and they stopped altogether. As the truck
emerged, dusk had been quelled by night.

There was now the pitch-black distance. For some time
we cut through it peacefully, until there was a setback.
The westbound lanes had been closed off for repairs,

and it was a question of slowing over four gears and snaking the trailer through a tight S-bend on to the two narrow lanes which were marked out for me on the eastbound carriageway. I would have preferred it if I had had more room, but I went through O.K. and laughed as I saw the back of the trailer clip a plastic bollard away into the darkness.

The traffic slowed. I came up behind another truck and was obliged to fidget between fifth and seventh gear. It was hard work. Cars in the other lane were cruising at sixty in a steady file; there were few gaps and I wasn't sure if the juggernaut could fit in. I decided to risk it. I looked in the mirror, waited for a fifty-yard gap and powered out, forcing the engine.

As soon as I was out there, I saw that it wasn't one truck, it was an unbroken line of a dozen, nose to tail. Half-way past the first one there was a line of cars up my back and the inside lane was blocked off. There was no way of opting out; I had to pass everything before I could pull in again.

Each time I passed a tractor, there were perhaps six inches between the wing-mirrors. The drivers looked across at me, I gave a professional nod. The sweat was on me again.

I wasn't quite sure what would happen if the road-works ended and two trucks had to take another S-bend side by side. I felt, rather than noticed, that Jade was silently awake on my shoulder. The noise of engines in proximity pounded the sealed cab with shock waves.

It was taking too long. I had lost count of the number of trucks I had passed. I willed the autobahn repairs to go on and on. I no longer glanced in the mirror to see the build-up of cars behind.

'Keep going,' Jade said suddenly, to relieve his own nerves; 'and go flat out.'

I was one and a half trucks from home when I saw the

flickering gold markers switch across to the other carriageway, perhaps five hundred yards ahead. My foot slackened on the accelerator.

'Keep going,' Jade warned. 'Put your indicators out.' He swung his legs down to sit on the bunk.

'We might not do it.'

'Flash the headlights.'

I did so.

Then with a rush, I seemed to be going at increased speed past the two trucks. I would manage it. I drew level with the cab of the front truck, I glanced over; the driver was enjoying a broad grin. I swept past. Two hundred yards, one-fifty. Lights flashed in my mirror.

'You're clear of him. Pull half-way over. Block both lanes off. Start braking. Gently. Drop a gear. Brake. Down again.' The engine screamed. 'Keep it dead straight. Down again. No, leave it for now. More brake. You've got both lanes. Drop another gear. Accelerate as soon as you're half-way through the bend. Go for the diagonal, straight as you can. Take both lanes. You'll bounce her but she'll hold.'

Jade watched the trailer through the mirror.

'Accelerate now!'

We bounced and jerked, I felt the weight swinging to one side, trying to escape, and then it came back again.

'Keep accelerating, use all the road. Pull her straight.'

I held on to the trailer.

'Good driving.' Jade slithered down into the passenger's seat. 'Flash your lights.'

'What for?'

'Because if the driver in the front truck hadn't have braked, we would have been off the road.'

I flashed the lights; an answering glare splashed off the mirror into my eyes. Cars started to pass us. The open road stretched black.

'Was it my fault? I suppose it was.' I felt weak.

'No one's fault. It was good driving. In an English truck, you can't see round if there's another trucker ahead of you. If I'd have been in the passenger's seat we could have edged out to take a look. As it was, you get out there and you're committed. If something takes your place on the inside, you've got to go on. It does just happen to be illegal though; it was a car lane. Where are we?'

'I've no idea.'

'We didn't go through the border at seventy-five, did we?'

'I don't think so.'

'No. That's Aachen. Over there to the right. It's about ten kilometres to the border.'

Jade reached into the bottom bunk for his briefcase, and fiddled through it. 'This won't take long. If you pull into the queue, I'll go over and get the papers stamped.'

I lost sight of Jade as he ran off along the line of trucks which stood with their engines idling in the lay-by outside Customs. I rested my arms on the wheel and felt chastened, lost in the job. I felt like patting the cab.

There was a tap on my door. I wound down the window and met the cheery face which had smiled at me two hundred yards before the S-bend.

'*Engländer? Ja? Zigarette?*'

'*Ja.*' I accepted the cigarette and a light.

'*Starker Lastwagen, was?*' The German looked the cab up and down.

'*Ja. Ja.* Er . . . *danke.*' I cocked my thumb back down the road and grinned sheepishly.

'*Danke? Nicht der Mühe wert. Gute Fahrt. Nach England?*'

'*Ja.*'

Jade was back below the driver's door, impatient.

'This is the guy who let us through, who braked.'

'Yeah?' Jade nodded absent-mindedly.

'*Starker Motor, was . . .* '

'Yeah well we'll be seeing you. *Auf Wiedersehen.*' Jade opened the cab door. 'Move over.'

The sandalled German walked away, clutching a sheaf of papers. I clambered across to the passenger's seat.

'Got your passport?'

'Yes.' I felt it in my pocket. Jade had already started up and was throwing the tractor from left to right, squeezing us out of the line of trucks.

'That was a nice guy.' I pondered. 'Quite human.'

'Yeah, they're all nice guys. They want to stand around and talk about trucks. This is a good one to talk about, you could waste half an hour showing it off.'

'It was good of him to give us the space on the bend.'

'It was professional. I'll do the same for him one day. It doesn't mean that he can stand around wasting my time.'

Jade had us free and accelerating towards the border post. We offered our passports. We were waved through. Jade slammed a cassette into the tape-player and pounded us on into night-time Belgium.

I watched the lights of the vehicles. Each driver was in his or her capsule, disturbed by a glare in the mirror and attentive to any unknown presence that came out of the darkness. Intimacy over, it was a matter of following each solitary rear-light into the pattern of red dots ahead, watching the pattern's constant flux, calculating and re-calculating one's own reference to the immediate future.

'How are you?' I asked Jade after we had passed through Brussels.

'I'll take us through, unless you want to drive.'

'No, that's all right. Once is enough, just for the experience. Thanks.'

'My pleasure; thanks for the company.'

Jewels

I HAD GOT OUT of bed and pulled my hat over my eyes and gone to the supermarket in search of something simple and canned which would match my appetite for life. I arrived at the check-out counter without having chosen anything; I had a vague feeling of guilt, as though it might be an offence to walk round a whole supermarket and end up with an empty basket.

The bloke in front of me had bread, cheese, tomatoes and lager; I admired. I went quickly back amongst the shelves and got bread, cheese, tomatoes and lager; and then I presented myself for reckoning.

I didn't have enough money. The bloke was pushing his food into a haversack. He caught my eye.

'Not enough money . . . ' I admitted.

'*J'en ai de trop. Puis on a des tomates quand même.*'

The bloke shovelled across some loose change as though it annoyed him and left the second bag of tomatoes to Caroline of the fast fingers, pink nylon coat and cash till.

'*Oui. Bon,*' I agreed.

We ate back in the kitchen, in between bits and pieces of communication. Luc was on holiday in England. He'd arrived the day before and was going back that night because he didn't like it. He lived in France, in the mountains. I put one or two belongings into a polythene bag and went with him.

I now lived in a room, washed in blue, from which I could see a miniature road down in the valley with cars that moved silently. But mostly I could see only blue and green; the blue of the sky and the green of the vast forest which hung on the opposite mountainside and crawled up as high as it was allowed.

That first morning, I stayed in my room, sitting in a chair, amazed at the height and the depth and the silence; not quite sure whether it was ponderous and awkward, or whether it was merely different and watching me. I felt like a cat in an unknown boudoir. I picked up a book, frantically, and read for two hours, looking up briefly whenever I turned the page. In the middle of the day I opened the window and smelt warm air. It was still somehow a bit distant to be real. I was grateful.

I put the book down, wearying of it. I tried to sketch the great jawbone of rock and its deep, green beard; framed as it was, safely, by the window. I couldn't quite manage the loop of the cables which fell across the valley and rose again towards the house. And there were thinner cables, with logs on them no bigger than the naked lead on the pencil; which suddenly gave stupefying scale to what was outside the window.

Close to me, there was a stomping and a crashing and a burping along the corridor; then murmurs through the wall and the soft cry of a girl in pleasure, and then silence.

I ought to come to terms with this place, make some arrangement with it.

I opened my door and looked along the corridor. None of the other rooms bothered with doors. I walked past various sleepers; a girl with dark, curly hair was awake and smiled. I smiled back and walked on downstairs, closing the main door behind me.

I knocked cautiously. There was no answer. I went into a large room. The remains of an extensive lunch were scattered over a long, wooden table, and this time there were three huge windows which looked out over the drop into the valley and through which the sun blazed in a solid curtain, shutting half the room into darkness.

I made coffee on the gas stove and picked at some bread and salad, feeling very much on stage in the glare of the sunlight. There was someone making love in the room over my head. I looked around me at the big, chaotic kitchen. There were four comfortable chairs in front of an immense fireplace which dominated the room. Two cats and a duck regarded me from a cushioned bench. Dozing flies were splayed over the walls like drawing-pins, others weaved in and out of the shade or dropped down on to the table to copulate quickly.

I advanced to a window. The valley heaved in the heat. Three old women were knitting, on a log by the side of the road. As I watched them, they glanced up and seemed to recognise me. And then I saw Luc, who had been lying on the grass and was now laughing as he pointed up the road towards the house.

I closed the kitchen door and stepped down into the front yard. I saw an axe lying in the dust and picked it up, leaning it against the wall of the house without knowing quite why, except that it made me feel that I was there and would recognise something when I came back.

I pushed open a small gate and climbed over a tree-trunk to get to the road. I strolled down, hands in my pockets, to see Luc.

'*Anglais*,' Luc explained as I stood bewildered in the flow of the women's chatter.

'*Ah . . .*' they choroused, '*Anglais*.' A reference all on its own. Luc smiled.

'No *sieste*?' he asked.

'No.'

'I will show you how we live.'

We left the women with much laughing on their part, which disconcerted me.

'Vegetables.' Luc stood on a rise and waved his arm over a field. 'Leeks, potatoes, beans, beetroot, peas, salad, radishes.' He looked to gauge my reaction.

'Very good. Do you have a tractor?' I managed to ask him with mime and gesticulation. Luc laughed.

'There is a horse,' he said; 'but you can never catch him. We've got shovels. The horse has just arrived. All this was the mountain, it was wild. We cleared it the first summer we were here; with shovels and with an old axe.'

I nodded. 'How many people?'

'Twelve people. And sometimes friends who come and think it is a holiday. Tourists are not much help.'

'It's a commune.'

'Perhaps.' Luc smiled. 'Perhaps just a farm.'

We walked through lines of vegetables and then climbed up the disused terraces; I glanced over my shoulder at the forest. I had thought that we might be nearer, but it had retreated silently. It must be two or three miles away, across a ravine which I couldn't see. I arrived, panting, at a wire fence.

'Chickens, ducks, geese, turkeys,' Luc introduced.

'There's a duck in the kitchen.'

'That's Napoleon. He likes to get away from the women.'

Luc unhooked the gate and we walked on, through an acre of cropped grass and weeds, past a hut. There was a sudden commotion, as if someone had shaken a cardboard box; a dozen hens piled out of the hut and sprinted towards us like berserk paddle-steamers. Luc went down to catch the leader and whipped her up by the legs, squalling and then she was fearfully still. He pulled aside the tail feathers.

'Worms.' He pointed. 'We'll have to spray them. We'll have to do it at dusk when they're all inside.'

'Yes,' I agreed sagely. Luc threw the hen across at her room-mates and they all became upset; ruffled and shrieking, they pecked spitefully at each other. Luc shook his head and motioned me back through the fence. We

54

stood watching as the hens furled their wings irritably and checked the ground in a half-hearted way, wary of each other and ever ready to flare into a quarrel. The cock, who had arrived too late, now flung himself stupidly at the wire in front of my legs, time and time again. Luc laughed. He opened the gate and the cock backed away to muster his dignity from the top of the dunghill.

Luc was bored with the tour. He rested one arm on the wire and watched my reactions.

'Pigs, cows, goats, rabbits, hay . . . ' He jerked his head in the direction of the farm buildings.

'All inside?' I asked.

'Yes, it's too hot at midday. They won't eat. Too many flies.'

'And you sell the milk?'

'Cheese. We sell it at the market on Saturday, down in the town. To buy axes and barbed wire. We can't make those yet.'

'What do you do about money?' I inquired.

'Simple. There isn't any. We spend what we make. In the summer we put some aside for the winter. All the money is kept in the kitchen dresser; you take what you want.'

'Does that work?'

'Yes. It's worthless. Sometimes we drink. Money always comes from somewhere.'

'You had money in London.'

'You need money in the city.'

'The others didn't mind?'

'Why should they? It was raining. No one else wanted to go to London. They thought I was mad.' Luc shrugged. I thought I saw a flash of anger in his eyes which he killed quickly. It was directed over my shoulder. I turned to look.

There was a very out-of-place man, dressed for the

town but taking an abnormal interest in the barn. Luc regarded him contemptuously. The man sauntered towards us with confidence.

'*C'est vous qui vendez du fromage?*'

'Yes, we sell cheese down in the house, if there's anyone awake.' Luc brushed him aside.

'*Merci.*' The man walked off.

'Who's that?' I asked.

'Police. Just checking up on the communists or anarchists or whatever they think we are this month. They've got nothing better to do than to file reports which make themselves seem important. We don't breed bombs at the moment. If you wait here, the others will be up soon to gather the hay.'

'O.K.'

Luc didn't encourage company. I sat on the step of the barn and watched him walk away up the path.

I was bothered by the heat at the same time as I became distracted by the noise of someone systematically destroying a shed with a sledgehammer. I looked across at the farm buildings but couldn't see anyone. I took off my shirt and went to investigate. It seemed to come from this shed here. I pushed open the door.

Some sort of goat glared at me evilly from a pen. I considered it and cast an eye into the adjacent pen. There was a large sow, sprawled across a floor of railway sleepers, dead to the world with her shoulders twitching in sleep and a mess of trampled greenery scattered around the sty. This was a peaceful setting. I grinned at the luxury of the sow.

There was an ear-splitting crash. I jumped back against the wall. The great billy-goat was already up on its hind legs again, towering over me for a moment and then plunging the horns down against the wooden planks of its pen. The two-inch thick wood splintered and smashed. This was a malicious animal. I backed towards the door and stared in shock at this tall, horned figure, rearing over its stall, eyes gleaming with hatred and the sheer joy of destruction, watching me victoriously before falling with all its force on to the ripped planking. It shuffled back, licking its lips quickly, having made its point. The sow grunted and twitched, yawned like a dog and rubbed her ear along a railway sleeper before sighing and closing her eyes again. I locked the door behind me.

There were two figures bouncing up the path towards the farm. There was a small fellow with overburdened trouser pockets which sagged down past his kneecaps, and a long, slim girl. They were obviously in love. She smiled and he grinned to reveal a set of very rotten teeth.

'*Salut.*'

'*Salut.*'

They were Voyou and Frédérique.

'*Bon. Au foin.* Work. The hay. *Faut sortir le bouc.*' Voyou looked at my alarm and laughed. 'Ah, you know the buck. Herbie. We must take him out to eat. Together it is not so bad.' Voyou laughed again and fetched two ropes.

'I don't like the *bouc.*' Frédérique wisely took herself off to one side.

'Right.' I adopted a business-like tone. Voyou marched into the pen and there was a holocaust of banging and cursing and shouting.

'*Ho . . . ho! Bordel de shiotte de merde . . .*' The buck appeared at a trot with Voyou hanging on to one rope. I got out of the way. The buck wasn't going to stop for anything. Voyou was already some five yards down the path, digging in his heels against the animal's acceleration.

'*Tiens!*' He waved the other rope at me as he skied through the dust behind the powerful shoulders. I caught him and grabbed the cord. The buck slowed.

'Strong, eh?' Voyou laughed.

The buck jerked us up the mountain at a good walking pace.

'*À gauche!*'

We dragged the lunatic off the track to a terrace on the left, and it walked calmly into the shade of the trees. The rope slackened. All three of us kept our eyes on each other but the buck seemed quiet enough. We reached a large circle of trampled grass and a long chain, staked into the earth. The buck paused. Voyou spoke to it, a long camouflaging monologue while he slowly approached and stroked its head. The buck became suspicious.

Voyou motioned to me to take hold of the horns while he attached the chain to its collar and untied the ropes. When he bent down to pick up the chain, his eyes flicking nervously, I realised that we were each as scared as the other.

The ring of the chain snapped shut over the collar and the buck exploded. I was astride it, then not astride it; Voyou had one horn in hand, then the other. The buck put his head down and wrestled. He was impossibly strong and devious. We were out of control.

'Run!' Voyou shouted, and we both ran ten steps and threw ourselves another yard. The buck charged after us, I glimpsed the enraged yet playful eyes, a foot away, the pointed horns lowered. And then, as I lay in the grass, heart pumping, the buck leapt up in the air and was choked backwards as the chain tightened and held.

'Mad.' Voyou laughed as he picked himself up. The buck, uninterested, sauntered round his domain.

Frédérique came up behind us. She carried three long wooden rakes. She shook her head in dislike of the danger. Voyou chided her.

We walked through the grass and climbed slowly up the mountain in the heat, towards the depthless blue sky; none of us said a word. We concentrated on the thump of our boots against the steep path and the itchy feeling as the sweat began to break out.

When we finally reached the terrace which had been

scythed the morning before, we sat, bowed over with the first bout of exhaustion; Voyou frowning at his own limitations, my legs peculiarly insubstantial in their weakness and Frédérique mopping her brow as she passed round the bottle of water. Half dreamily, we watched the others trail up towards us. Voyou gave them names: Henri out at the front, Marc, Pierre, Annie, Paul, Belline, Cathy, Christine, Françoise; small figures even at a hundred yards, each climbing according to his or her own pace with rakes and ropes and pulleys, the stretch of blue sky splashed artificially over the mountain ranges and the forest strangely colourless in the afternoon haze.

Voyou detached himself from the ground and picked up his rake. Frédérique had already started working, alone at the top of the terrace, her straw hat pushed back on her head, her back rising and falling with the strokes of the rake. Voyou patted her as he went past. He bent and gathered a handful of hay, examining it sceptically. Frédérique worked on; already she had the hay forming into a roll, drawing it towards her legs methodically and moving sideways; throwing the head of the rake away from her, leaning and straightening as she pulled it back into her feet.

'*Bordel . . .*'

Henri arrived next to me, a dead cigarette hanging from the corner of his mouth. He threw down a mass of ropes and the clanking pulleys and was quick away, checking the teeth of his rake as he walked to the other end of the terrace. He pitched himself into the work and this small tier was half stripped by the time the others arrived in a bunch, spreading themselves out in a line of eleven, pulling the roll of hay down the mountain, bending and sweating in silence; moving across from left to right and back again, slowly drawing themselves out of the siesta and into the rhythm of their muscles.

The roll arrived at the edge of the terrace. The ropes

were laid out in threes and the hay was compressed tight against the shins; building up a small bale, folding in the ends, smashing the stems tight together, reaching for more hay, piling it up to the thighs until there was an impossibly large armful to be carried across to the ropes; a small hillock of hay, six mounds of hay and Henri already throwing the unused ropes over his shoulder and moving up the mountain to the next level after a swig at the water-bottle. The others looking up and checking, Voyou nodding at me and wiping a hand across his brow, waving them on up in a jovial slang. I light-headed with the work and the heat and the astonishing drop over my shoulder which wasn't to be dwelt on but was always there, deep and far and hard to focus whenever it caught me raising my eyes from the stubble. It asked me to fall and I turned my head back to what was solid at my feet.

'*Bon.*' Voyou flung the ropes over the top of the hay and threaded them through the wooden eye, sitting on the ground with his feet tensed against the bale. '*En avant les femmes.*'

Frédérique knelt on top of the hay and bounced up and down as Voyou pulled the cords tighter and tighter. When he was satisfied, he tied the rope to the eye and tucked the ends into the bale. '*Bon.*' He tested his packing and kissed Frédérique. '*Puis les cinq autres?*' he suggested to my inactivity.

'*On y va?*' I looked at the little girl beside me, who had smiled earlier from her bed. Little, but not young; large green eyes and a frizz of black, curly hair. She was dark from the sun and had the body of an animal. She laughed at my stare and took me over to the hay.

She made a great show of climbing on to the bale and bouncing it flat. I had trouble fixing the cords, I needed more than two hands and she held the rope tight while I made the knot. She had bitten her nails to the quick, I noticed, and she loved to flirt. I felt awkward in front of her, sure that she was laughing at my fumbling. Something in her beguiled me and mocked this effect at the same time.

'Christine?' I wondered.

'*Ah oui?*' She let her eyes open wide, playing the child. She was Luc's lover; the aristocrat, the oldest girl on the farm. '*Oui?*' she repeated, putting her head on one side. '*Le prochain? On y va, m'sieur?*'

We moved across to the next bale and again she was coy. I felt a strange reproach from Frédérique, a few feet away, while Voyou joked. Christine, too, felt the hostility. She scowled. I kept my eye on the ropes rather than the cutaway T-shirt.

We finished binding the hay and the girls were all for moving on up. Voyou would have none of it. '*On en fume une.*' He waved them away and settled with me in the shade, looking out over the valley. The girls walked off separately, having nothing to say to each other. Voyou and I smoked a cigarette.

'*Beau, eh?*' Voyou nodded across at the mountain peaks and the forest. I wanted to ask about Christine, but Voyou wasn't interested in gossip. He knew a lot about their idealism, which was more important. The people would have to adapt, and if they didn't like it they should go away. If he wanted a cigarette in peace, he would have one. We smoked. Voyou pointed out the name of a mountain or a wild flower. The cigarette finished, he rolled forward on to his feet.

The next terrace was perhaps twice as large, and the others were more in tune with the work; much in couples, exchanging remarks and fooling. Voyou and I found space in the line and began peeling away the hay from the stubble. Voyou started a song and Christine was there at my elbow, laughing and trilling. I found myself humming some old tune which occasionally fitted the French chorus; it made me smile. The song was rolling and sentimental, I had no idea where it came from. Most of the music I liked had been jangling, discordant, frenetic. Now I hummed peacefully to fit the rise and fall of the rake. I smiled carelessly at my introversion, and, by the time I had done that, we had left one curling wave of hay above us and there was another sweet-smelling tangle creeping up to my knees.

I leaned on my rake and looked along the line of hats and shoulders and sunburned skin. It was like a propaganda poster. Sweat and song. I confided in Voyou.

'Perhaps.' Voyou grinned.

But, with the moment's watching, I had fallen behind and was dug in the ribs by Christine, chiding me playfully. Henri, out on the wing, discarded his rake and went for the ropes, anxious to be on with it and get it done, the same dead cigarette stuck to his lip.

'Bof! Fou, lui; il est fou.' Christine was ugly in her dislike. Voyou baited her and she became the coquette, inviting my eyes to the dance. Frédérique murmured and Voyou calmed her affectionately.

All this was strange and sudden to me, stuck there on the side of a mountain, becoming at home first with the instrument that was my body, getting to know how far it was comfortable to lean and at what point the trickle of sweat annoyed me so much that I had to break my rhythm, lean on my rake and wonder if we were ever to stop. It was better to work though, to keep the rake bucking over the stubble towards you with the stems snapping and the blades of hay rustling. I was determined to work, to draw up as much hay as I could; it annoyed me to leave any strands lying uselessly on the ground, I jerked hard on the rake, time and time again; I heard nothing but the scratching of the wood along the stubble and the stamping of my feet as I put them down beside each other and swayed forward with my back bent, shirt sleeves flapping and hair an uncomfortably hot wig which perched uneasily over my blank mind. I heard Voyou as if from a distance.

'*On fume.*'

'No, I'll go on; get this finished.'

'You want to be a hero?' Voyou tapped me, looking into my eyes shrewdly, like a doctor, questioning. I realised that the others were all sitting under a tree and that Voyou was the only one working. I felt a shifting sickness.

'It is very hot,' Voyou said respectfully, 'you are not used to the sun. Take care.'

Under the tree was cool. We ate bread and ham. I stayed there and watched them from the shade when they went back to work, the most graceful machines, their foreign chatter spilling across the glare to me. Christine had the smallest body. I had smelt it when she passed me the food. It was a simple desire I had for her. She saw me looking at her breasts.

For two weeks I watched them and her, wondering how I should fit in; slightly alienated by the way in which the farm seemed to run itself, slightly clumsy towards the work and the people, often lost and left behind. I didn't know what I was doing or why I was doing it except that something inside me responded to the atmosphere of creation. None of them ever looked back, or analysed, or told me what to do. They all went forward in a surge; a massively extrovert, creative gesture. Unselfconscious, erotic. Christine watched me go with them. Sometimes this would check me back into being an individual, pin me down with my own personal desire for her which she recognised and played on.

I threw myself out into the farm. I knocked up a couple of ramshackle shelves for my bedroom. I announced that their treatment of the sow was criminal and that I would undertake this responsibility myself. I instituted a small patch of lawn in front of the house which became known as Hyde Park. And I found that I worked very well as a roof-building team with Voyou and Frédérique. I covered up my vulnerability to Christine.

The beauty became more strange. I had had no experience of being up at dawn, not on a summer's morning, not unless it was still part of the night and daylight was suddenly there by accident. But now I found myself up at four o'clock, shivering sleepily in the kitchen over a bowl of milky coffee.

We would wander slowly up the mountain through the wet grass, now grey, to the highest terraces. I would follow the sweep of the scythes with a rake, spreading the heavy dew-drenched clumps into a thin coverlet; with the sighing swish of the blades and the clank of the whetstone the only commotion to disturb the calm.

Scything was the one skill I couldn't manage; it was something primitive that left me angry with envy and in awe of the beauty of the motion.

Silent, wet-through to the thighs, the six men moved peacefully in a line across the terrace, swinging from side to side most effortlessly, pivoted at the waist; the grass bowing gracefully over the silver blades and sliding dead to the ground. I was without the key to this self-contained beauty. The scythers moved against the cold wall of the mountain. I turned and saw the sun hopping cautiously in and out of the opposite crags until it suddenly lifted itself up one bit further and blazed out at us.

The pace slackened then, and Henri took advantage of Voyou's match; they lit a cigarette. They finished the line and wound their way light-footed down the path towards the clang of milk churns at the farm, each one enclosed in his own pride.

This was the grass we would gather in as hay in two days' time, when the sun had dried it.

The cable rumbled slightly. I shielded my eyes against

the fading sun and looked back up the mountain. A tiny Marc wheeled the bale of hay along to the first stanchion and held it. He whistled and raised his arm. I waved.

Marc gave the bale a push. It started its journey down from the terraces, swinging from side to side, held by the pulley as it rushed down the wire.

I called to the dog and lifted the previous bale out of the way. I was surprised at how light the work had become.

The cable jumped wildly. I moved aside and the ninth bale whacked fast into the buffer. It bounded back and leapt off the wire. I waved again at Marc and the cable was already rumbling with the next hundredweight. Luc approached, huge and grimy and tired.

'You want the cable?' I offered him a rest. Luc nodded.

I stood before the bale. I concentrated on it for a moment. Then I dug my hands under the two outside ropes, hauled it up to my knee and jerked it back over my head, letting it drop on to my shoulders. I staggered for balance and arranged the weight evenly; I started off on the last two hundred yards to the barn.

This was the final exhausting task of the day, this carrying of the twenty-odd bales when you were bent double with accumulated fatigue and a false step sent the hay tipping to one side unless you danced quickly back underneath its weight. Once it dropped, the hateful bulk of it, you hadn't the energy or the will to get it up again. It was a defeat.

I carried six bales into the barn and then sat on the steps, waiting for Luc to arrive with the last one. It was a beautiful evening. It was often a beautiful evening, resting contentedly after the work.

A duck lurched round the corner of the barn and stood for a moment. It quacked. I observed it. It became interested, it straightened its neck and looked over at me; then it scuffled its beak in the mud under the tap.

I sat on the step, wiped-out, dusty; enjoying this late afternoon lull. The hay was finished for the day, the heat of the open sun was climbing slowly up the wall of the pigsty. Every muscle ached. I stank.

My neighbour quacked again. I nodded in faint agreement. The duck rolled towards me, muttering to itself quite seriously like one of those old women with their shopping on top of a London bus.

'Well, Napoleon . . . '

The duck stopped in surprise. He wagged his tail nervously and stretched out his neck.

'What's happened to your mistresses?' I asked. It was Napoleon's wont to spend the late afternoon rolling in the dust with a mistress, but now he stamped up gruffly and sat down at my feet. The chattering died away. We had little to say to one another. There were no problems. Tomorrow would pass in much the same way as today had done, for both of us. We would both be awake at dawn, we would both eat well and spend our time plodding round the farm and the hillside. There wasn't much to worry about, nothing unexpected could happen; one could only agree with the slow and inevitable pace.

Napoleon stood up and shook his feathers. He muttered again and broke into exclamation. I peered at the egg in front of my boot. Ah well, it wasn't Napoleon.

Whoever it was disappeared back round the corner. I was deeply touched at the trust placed in me by the unknown duck, leaving its egg, still warm, by the side of my great boot. It was miraculous.

'*Attention!* . . . *hola* . . . ' Luc stumbled down the path, out of control, with a huge tuft of badly roped hay falling from side to side across his shoulders. He was so bent that the only brown skin visible was at kneecap level against the splits in his trousers. ' . . . Where am I? . . . where's the path? . . . *merde* . . . '

'Stop!' I ordered.

66

Luc stopped, the hay continued, the ropes slipped; and there was a new, thick, perfumed mat over the dirt. Luc painfully pulled himself straight.

'The buck get out?' He searched around him for any emergency that might need his strength.

'No, no. A duck laid this egg. Just here. While I was sitting.'

Miracles always sound ridiculous in replay. Luc looked at me. I knew how far he had carried that hay to be able to cross off another number on the chart. And how it was a wonderful part of the day, most serene with the fatigue and the stilwarm sun, to stroll unencumbered instead of with the heavy, torturing hundredweight of prickly grass and stems.

I bent to try and skim off such hay as hadn't touched the ground or fallen into the puddle from the tap. I gathered up two armfuls and threw them into the barn, stepping carefully over the egg each time.

'Leave it,' Luc advised from the step. 'It'll do for the pigsty.'

'Some of it's all right.'

'I wouldn't bother with it. We've done twenty-two bales today.' He held out the tobacco pouch and papers.

'Twenty-three makes . . . ' I hesitated.

'Four hundred. Twenty tons. Well, that's three hundred and ninety-nine and a half, and a duck egg.' Luc smiled.

'How much do we need?'

'Another two hundred and a half.'

I rolled a cigarette, considering the egg.

'Will we make it?'

'Who knows? We've got to. So presumably we will. The only point in making it is so that you can sit on a step and have a duck come up to you and lay an egg. Six hundred is only a number.'

Last night the arguments had raged. We had done

twenty-something bales for the sixth day running; scything at dawn, sleeping two hours at midday, raking all afternoon and finishing off the milking at ten in the evening before we ate. They were sick of it. They hated it. They had been doing it on and off for two months. But winter was seven months and five feet of snow.

Luc thought that the farm defined its own needs; squabbling was a privilege reserved for you if you ever had any energy left at the end of the day, which he never did. So he picked up the alarm clock, mumbled a good night which got lost in the hubbub, and went to bed. The grumbling went on, but they knew that they'd be up the next morning at four. Not because of Luc, but because if one person thought it was worth doing, then it was worth doing for everyone.

We waited for the energy to seep back into us. Luc stood up and took the duck egg down to the kitchen. I stayed up at the farm, waiting for Christine.

Of all the evening chores, I preferred to milk the goats. They were the most tender animals, sitting in the straw, ruminating over their afternoon's feed: Groslolo, Petit Chien, Alberte and Bosquez; I knew most of their names by now, the thirty of them in three generations, the old coughing as they chewed, the young more inquisitive, resting their heads on my shoulder as they waited to be emptied. They liked affection. The warm, fetid stable was familiar at the end of the day.

I waited for Christine to bring the churn up from the house. She usually marked herself down to work with me. I listened to her gossip, watching her supple body and her hands on the long dugs of the goats.

She would often flirt outrageously with me in the fields, throwing hay and calling to me; but she was always serious when we milked together. Unfortunately, her seriousness was more poignant. I wanted her; I was infatuated. Making love would have dissolved the tension that was stifling the atmosphere. But we wouldn't make love. I had come to learn why not. She had given herself to Luc. She had very little of herself left and was weakened further by the demands of living on the commune. She fought desperately to be light-hearted and friendly with the other women, but, from the depths of their secure couples, they regarded her with suspicion.

Because she wasn't in a couple. Luc wanted her to join the women's club much as he joined the men's club; except that the women didn't have a club and they were each joined to their lover, or two lovers in the case of Françoise. And Luc didn't want Christine joining him; he was content to muck his way round the commune, often choosing to work alone in a massively dozy fashion, brooding over aims and ideals. He smiled condescendingly at her nervous giggles; he was the only person who never had to do his own washing.

He had perhaps the natural aloneness of a leader, which he could never be bothered to use. Not that it would have got him anywhere; he would have been drummed out of court. Luc had no time for groaners and, in the name of libertarian principles, he made himself inaccessible to criticism. He gave freely of everything, except himself. Christine deserved better; she was defenceless and suffered from a natural inclination to panic when she missed her footing. She grabbed at any straw, often viciously defiant of the sterile block of common sense over which the other women perched. She crashed and leapt from mood to mood, childish and unstable, capricious and vacant.

I adored her. A world of such people would be a mess of jewels; I thought that the commune should be able to afford at least one.

It was exasperating how she always grabbed for the best piece of meat at dinner, her blood raised in challenge against the dull communal power bloc; how she served the wine into the glasses of those she thought were on her side; how Luc, Voyou and myself always ended up with vast plates of food before the others had considered emerging from their tiredness; it was ridiculous the way she distributed these invitations to dislike; she was insufferable, utterly careless and then quite capable of mortifying herself with sham apology whenever she met her come-uppance.

Part of her isolation must have been that Luc had no wish to take her in hand. It rather disrupted his self-imposed communal brooding to have someone so avaricious for personal attention hanging on his elbow. He refused to protect her. So, out of the panic that came over her whenever she considered herself – and she had a great stock of severely Catholic guilt – she would put on her secret eye make-up and enrol my infatuation to prop her up. She got desperate when Luc brushed her unhappiness to the side of his universal platter, and she felt a sudden void.

I was mesmerised by her; she was a divine fool. I cleared my head. The poultry needed feeding.

I shambled round to the granary and collected the bucket of grain. The hens followed me round the wire expectantly. I waited. I tried to be fair. The hens bitched so aggressively that the other poultry often got nothing to eat. So I delayed, keeping the bucket hidden. The hens lost interest and returned to the dungheap.

Round the corner of the hut came the species of self-propelled Indian head-dress, stamping its feet, its wings dragging stiffly across the ground and a long, obscene finger of red skin flapping from side to side over its beak. It made a noise like a horse sneezing, or a slow-pumping steam engine. It moved haughtily in its strange, instinctive performance; its wattle became a most beautiful deep magenta.

I scattered the grain over the wire. The hens rushed in a

mass from the dunghill and fought each other bitterly for the corn. The turkey was battered this way and that, hopping to retain his balance. Finally, as the hens dispersed, he cast a sad eye around him at the grainless earth; he lowered his wing feathers, paused for a moment, and uttered a dispirited snuffle. He danced beautifully, but he was always too slow to get anything to eat; as bemused as a timid bourgeois by the lack of etiquette.

It wasn't the end of his troubles. Suddenly there was a rush of white, like newspaper caught up by the wind, tormented and flung around. The paranoid brothers. Coming from nowhere, going nowhere – a swirling foursome of geese ran up in a tornado, tugged this way and that by the tiny madness in their heads. They charged to left and to right, wheeling uphill and downhill in a thoughtless eddy, barking and howling, so excited by feeding-time that they never bothered to look down for the food. And the dust cleared as they disappeared over some short horizon, leaving the turkey hunched under his flap, eyes blinking; an old tramp who finds his familiar shelter next to a new motorway.

'*Bonsoir.*' Christine caught me unawares. She dropped the churn at my feet and put her head against my arm mockingly, like a child. I was only sometimes sure that she wasn't being genuine. Once, when just the two of us had untied the bales and spread the hay into the corners of the barn, I asked her to make love. How seriously she considered it. I joked because of the pause. She took the suggestion as a compliment. She was pleased with compliments; she said I was kind and she meant it.

I took the churn. She followed me into the stable. The bloated goats stood, winking and chewing; their ears flicked nervously. She stroked Alberte between the horns and the goat bent its head in ecstasy. She murmured at it.

I handed her a bucket, anxious to be on with the work. She laughed at me.

We were in among the goats, kneeling on the straw, pulling the milk from the breasts. I lost her in the rhythm. She was subdued this evening, moving quietly from animal to animal on the other side of the stable. Occasionally I caught sight of the small area of brown back that showed as she knelt.

I milked methodically, odd memories cropping up. When the cows escaped one night and Voyou roused me for the chase. We were leaning against the repaired fence, a bit liquored after the dinner guests. We breathed deeply and stared at the moonlit horizon of white-topped peaks and Luc bet Voyou five francs that Christine was a better fuck than Frédérique. All of which kept him and Voyou in jovial dispute on the way back to bed; myself weaving behind them, tepid with camaraderie.

Bosquez shifted and looked round at me as I fumbled clumsily with her breasts. I concentrated on the matter in hand.

Above the ammonia smell of the stable, Christine's perfume reached across, and when she wasn't wearing any there was still the smell of her body.

Then there were the cries of the girls around the top of the house during the siesta sprawl and before the deep exhausted crash every night. I knew how Christine was in her excitement, I had lived through it often, she was only a wall away; the crocus fluttering open and the amazement for which she compressed herself and sprang.

I went across to the churn to empty the bucket. Outside, the rabbits scrambled over each others' bodies in immediate races of energy; the ducks dabbled discreetly through their mud. I looked back at Christine. The milking was almost finished. We worked quickly together.

She was self-conscious; as now, when she shook the final drops of milk from Alberte and, standing up, saw me looking at her. We both had the air of being trapped, finding each other physically oppressive – she knowing what her attraction caused, I worried at my intensity. It had to remain hidden, or played with. It was a routine by now, as much as washing out the buckets and carrying the churn back to the house.

It became obvious to the other people on the commune; that there was something unresolvable between us. These other people were now, to me, strangely lifeless bystanders on the periphery. Christine liked the public gaze, she was used to it; she could flit in amongst the cardboard figures or hide away down the long wooden table.

I began to look at her critically.

It hurt her. The flirting became less ludicrous and more bitter. We were both tired of it; it was how we had started and the habit dragged on.

She was still very much the outsider. No one wanted to work with her; Luc chose to be away on his own in some distant corner of the farm. He left her to work in the garden.

I veered away into roofing the new stable with Voyou and Frédérique. Christine was in the vegetable garden, hour after hour, a tiny and solitary figure, bending over the weeds and forking through the strawberries. I watched her from the roof. And Voyou watched me.

'We'll have to get another woman,' Voyou grinned. I shrank like a wounded animal. 'We'll stick an advert in the newspaper.'

Voyou spun a tile over in his hand, gauging the size and the shape and where it would fit.

'In the newspaper?'

'That's where they come from.'

I put down the pile of slate on a beam and smiled quizzically at the little fellow's sense of humour. Voyou was practical; hands chipped and swollen from the stone, hair dry and stiff with cement. He rarely appreciated flights of fancy. I laughed. Frédérique lugged a bucket of water towards us, balancing on the edge of the roof. Voyou's eyes lit up in admiration.

'She's a good one. *Eh, ma biche?*' he called.

'What?' She smiled at him; she was suspicious but ready for him.

'You see?' He took the bucket from her; he was proud of her. He tweaked her waist and she slapped him away.

'Get on with your work.' She turned to fill the next bucket. Voyou reached for the trowel.

'She came from the newspaper.'

'Bullshit,' I said.

'It's true. It's true,' Voyou pleaded, laughing, 'ask her. Frédérique? How did you come here? Tell him.'

'I saw the message in the newspaper and I came to see what was here.' She smiled.

'You see!' Voyou was overjoyed. 'And it was the same with Henri and Françoise, Pierre ... ' he paused, counting. 'How did Belline get here?'

Frédérique considered. 'I think she was a friend of Paul's brother.'

'Yes.' Voyou nodded excitedly. 'Then she was sleeping with Henri and Marc took her when he came back. Yes, that's it.'

'How did you two end up together?' I asked Frédérique.

'I had to sleep with him. It was either that or I slept in the kitchen. It was difficult.'

I could see her smile as she bent over the tap. Voyou exploded.

'Bof! I was free and happy until she took over the bed. Now my life's a complete misery.'

'Hah!' She threw half a bucket of water up at us. We hopped out of the way across the rafters.

'You see!' Voyou grinned. 'I can't even masturbate any more.'

'You can tonight, my love,' she offered him.

'We'll see ... ' he shook his finger knowingly. He

74

turned, intent on my problem. 'We'll put another advert in. It's simple.'

'How did Christine get here?' I asked, carelessly.

'She's an old friend of Luc's,' Voyou answered, carelessly. 'I like her,' he glanced across at Frédérique's back, 'but . . . ' He shook his hand as if it was burning. 'It's difficult for her. She doesn't fit.'

'Luc doesn't help her.'

'Luc is Luc.' Voyou nodded. 'Take her,' he said curtly. 'Masturbation gets a bit boring, perhaps she finds that as well.'

'I'm in love with her,' I confessed.

'What's the difference?' Voyou slapped a trowel of cement down on the stone and followed it with the slate. We worked for another half-hour and went for the midday meal.

During the siesta, I dozed in and out of dreams, a book open on the pillow; I had been on page 117 for a fortnight. The room and the forest were just as dreamy when my eyes opened; it was this terrible story of cosseted decay, *The Magic Mountain*; well, it could fester in a far corner of the room. I threw it away, and heard Christine pleading with Luc. Mumbling my own point of view, I shuffled back into sleep.

I was the last to arrive up at the hay. It was a pressing, weary day. We worked in silence. The flies made everyone irritable; they were monstrous, half bluebottle, half hornet, hugging the dungstains on clothes, horrible to look at but rarely bothering to sting. If it was a good day, they went unnoticed. On a bad day, they were the nuisance that kept you on edge.

'If this was a Hollywood film, there wouldn't be any bastard flies.' Even Voyou was set in ill-humour.

'If this was an English film,' I thought, 'we'd only have one bastard token goat and we wouldn't be in this boy scout camp in the first place.'

We worked slowly and listlessly. After an hour and a half we had roped eight bales and the pace had braked to a crawl. Only Henri, speeding along on his manic application, and Christine, who was glad to have Luc with her for once, kept us guiltily at it. It was getting late. We would soon lose half our number to the cows and the kitchen.

'*Pas de mouches.*' Voyou looked up at the sky and across at Marc.

'*Ah oui.*' Marc looked up the mountain.

'*On a encore combien de terrasses?*'

'*Encore deux. Deux grandes.*'

'*Ça fait dix-huit.* Eighteen bales.'

'*Peut-être.*'

'Shit,' I expressed myself phlegmatically.

'*Merde,*' Voyou translated.

'It's going to rain; the flies have gone.' Luc ambled across, as limp as a rag doll. Being the largest, he was the most destroyed by the humidity.

'Ah good . . . ' I foresaw days of peace and quiet. Voyou laughed.

'*On attaque?*'

I looked up in alarm. I hadn't the willpower to attack anything.

But we worked fast, so fast that it didn't bear thinking about, drawing the energy from worry and even the petty dislikes that floated around us. I found myself working in all kinds of combinations: kneeling on the hay while Frédérique tightened the ropes; completing a bale from start to finish in seven minutes with Henri, whom I saw smile; fighting over the debris in the bottom corner of the terrace with Annie, our rakes colliding and tangling . . .

'Leave it . . . ' Pierre shouted. The sky was clouding over and we went further up, scrambling through the needle brush, throwing the rakes ahead of us; I pulled Annie up by the arm; and this terrace was already

76

gathered in its rolls, a turbulent sea, the fresh breeze burrowing under the hay, lifting it slightly and carrying the grasses a few feet. Voyou was marching across towards the path, frowning in anger. Not enough ropes.

'I'll go.' I turned and was off, skidding down the mountain, half sideways, crashing from terrace to terrace with jolts that shook me from the ankle to the back of my neck, one arm held out behind me, leaning back like a ski-turn; then suddenly head over heels, losing the world except for the scratch of the stubble on my face, but up at the end of the somersault and charging on again in fast hectic disaster until the ditch by the road came up and knocked the breath out of me with one crude swipe.

I picked myself up and limped, thanking God it hadn't been a tree. I inflated slowly, as my ribs let me, each gasp for breath a little longer; then the barn was in front of me, the sky already darkening, the ropes hanging quietly from their nails, just inside the door.

I stopped in the darkness. A long way away a door creaked to and fro; I caught the impression of it above the noisy thumping of my heart and the feeling of sickness in my stomach. When I noticed it again, I snatched up the ropes and began the long climb back to where I had been before.

They took the ropes from me without saying a word and I lay on my back until the first rain spotted down. When I pulled myself up, there was Voyou, streaming with sweat, hay-dust blackening the furrows in his forehead, calling me off to where the two cables met. And we went diagonally across the mountain, jumping ditches and jogging over the already razed fields, the bales humming past us on the cable.

'*Attend un moment,*' I gasped.

'*On attend pas . . .* ' Voyou shouted. '*On attend pas Godot ici; on est anarchiste, on attend rien.*'

It was good to be that exalted; with the first bits of rain

whipping down, early guests mounting the adrenalin. The long run across the flat to the end of the first cable; beginning to feel cold, seizing the bales and unhooking them, dragging them across to the second cable, looking down the empty wire almost into the barn itself on the other side of the white strip of dusty road. And there I could see Pierre and Marc, running down the road to the cable's end, Marc waving Pierre on past to fetch the old truck. There was no time to carry the bales one by one.

The sky was hovering, the wind had dropped and the clouds were building up behind some invisible dam.

'Go!' Voyou shouted. I ran with the bale to the first tall stanchion and shoved it off on its own, wishing it something like a safe journey, watching it recede until Voyou ran past to send another bale in quick succession.

'That'll make him work . . . ' Voyou grinned, and we ran back to grab two more, unhitching them and dragging them across, almost in a fury against Marc.

'It's not raining very hard.'

'It will.' Voyou spoke over his shoulder as he launched his second bale. 'Shit! And fuck! And fuck it all!' He hopped up and down in a rage. I escorted my bale down towards the stocky figure. Voyou banged his fist on the wire. 'It's jumped. The cable's off. I'll have God's balls for this! You bastard!' He clenched his fist at the sky.

The cable was slack, indifferent; it kissed the ground just past the second stanchion.

'We're screwed.'

As if to spite us, another bale cruised to a halt against the dozen waiting on the end of the first cable. We regarded it with distaste. We were interrupted by a whistle from below. Voyou turned and shrugged expansively. He waved his arms forlornly from side to side, crossing them in the air. We heard the truck labouring up the mountain road.

The storm was black. The towering jawbone was shut

78

off from the sun by the heavy cloud which was welling in from the other end of the valley and creeping up over the hills behind us. It was cold now, and it would be down on us soon. It was desperate bad luck. We were defeated. The hay was not safe. Voyou snorted in disgust and spat; I sank in a crouch.

'*Bon.* The tarpaulin.' Voyou shrugged.

'Oh, there's a tarpaulin?' I looked up.

'Of course.'

We dragged it out from behind a ruined wall.

'That's all right then.' I rubbed my hands.

'It's disgusting.' Voyou shook his head. 'If you do something, you want to get it finished. It's the principle of it, not the hay.' He kicked out at a bale.

And indeed, when we had finished piling them up, had waited for a late straggler and had secured the tarpaulin with heavy rocks, we were joined by Christine, Luc and the other girls, all of whom seemed gloomy; and the gloom lasted as we filed down the mountain and sat in the kitchen. I couldn't understand it. Compared to where we were at five o'clock, bowed under apathy, we had worked wonders; and the bales were dry.

I left the others in the kitchen. I went upstairs to change my wet clothes. I stood at the open window and looked across the darkened valley. The sky was completely black; the rain had stopped and it was most calm. I switched on the light and returned to the window, drawing in deep breaths of the rich damp smell that rose from the earth. I heard the sound of a record from the kitchen, of the windows being shut and bolted. I was prompted into securing my wooden shutters, although it wasn't necessary; the wind had dropped and the storm must have gone somewhere else. It was best to make sure. The shutters might bang in the night.

The next time I was *compos mentis*, I found myself

staggering away from the window, my eyes straining through a thick gloom and my mind recovering from a violence of sound. It seemed to me as if someone had picked up the heavens and ripped them across from corner to corner. It was like being trapped in a biscuit tin under the boot of some giant.

As my senses crawled back, I was sitting on the bed. The lights had gone out and somewhere at the back of the house a window broke. It was a brilliant scattering of bells over the silence.

I wondered what had happened. My first reaction was that I might be the least injured and in a position to help the others.

I ran downstairs and threw open the door to the kitchen.

They moved slowly, as if they were in a dream sequence about death. They didn't look at me. Steam was pouring out of the untended kettle. Marc was moving from left to right, Françoise staring blankly out of the window. Voyou turned the page of a newspaper and knocked some ash off the end of his cigarette.

'What about closing the door?' Frédérique called from the fireplace. It was so normal.

I felt as if I had walked into another world. The thunder and lightning had perhaps happened only to me. I closed the door and smiled uneasily. No one took any notice.

But Christine was huddled in a corner of the bench in a tight little ball, and she was terrified.

It happened again, in slow motion. A brilliant flash of light transfixed us all. I saw lines in Christine's face that I had never seen before. The thunder stumbled drunkenly towards us and stamped hard on our heads.

Christine fidgeted violently, longing to move or tremble or scream, but ashamed to break the indifference. And yet we *were* afraid, somewhere. There was a tension. No one was touching anyone else. We hung around the room, lingering over each act, wary lest the thunder took us unexpectedly. Voyou was looking through the newspaper in a stubborn way; newspapers never interested him. Henri chipped at a piece of wood. Cathy was knitting and Frédérique leaning against the fireplace – each of us alone and in touch with our concentration, feeling a world of power which we could in no way influence. We waited.

When the storm rolled past, an enhanced banality filled the void. Voyou conveniently came to the end of his paper, Cathy held up her knitting and regarded it critically. Henri checked whether the piece of wood had become a tooth for his rake.

Christine shook herself and marched across the room to the record-player. She realised that once again she had been stupid in front of us all; the storm had pillaged the electricity. She sat down next to Luc, biting her nails and whispering to him. She harried him into leaving the room; he followed her out of the door sluggishly.

There was suddenly nothing to do. The room was gloomy without electric light. We weren't equipped to waste time. We found it hard to amuse ourselves. The atmosphere was claustrophobic. Outside the windows the rain teemed down. We watched it; we smoked cigarettes. There was a whisper of conversation, nobody wanted to talk. Henri went off to his workshop. Françoise went upstairs with Pierre; Marc and Belline also went to bed. For me, bed lacked something; anyway, I was marked down to milk the cows with Voyou.

Voyou slid down the bench and opened the backgammon board. In the half-light, the dice slammed to and fro. We had the same skill, but Voyou always won. This was so established that nowadays we played only when Voyou wanted to cheer himself up and I didn't mind allowing him the wherewithal.

Frédérique hung over us. She wanted his attention. She complained about the noise. Voyou spread the newspaper over the table, which deadened the sound. She felt neglected. He ignored her. She started preparing the vegetables for dinner.

We played three games. Voyou duly won three games. He felt sufficiently full of himself to approach the vegetables. He placated Frédérique. Conversation started again in the room as he prodded into her reserve, simultaneously joking and humble.

I looked out at the rain. I folded the backgammon board and wandered across the room. As usual, Paul was playing patience; the cards spread out in front of him. I watched the slow, careful movements of his large hands. Paul frowned intently. He was always momentarily perplexed at the fall of each third card, and he broke into smiling self-congratulation as it fitted into one of his runs. The game brought him a simple enthusiasm; he murmured with pleasure as he came to the end of the pack and turned the cards over to go through them again.

'How's it going?' I asked.

'Good.' Paul stared at the upturned card and grunted in mild disapproval.

'It seems to work out about one time in five.'

'Yes?' Paul looked up and wondered. He looked down at the table again and puzzled his way through the remaining cards; he arrived at the end of the pack and not one card had fitted in. He muttered.

'Have to start again . . . ' I laughed.

Paul picked up the pack and put the bottom card on the top. He started again; turning the cards over in threes, and fitting them in with pleasure.

'That's cheating,' I pointed out.

'What is?' Paul's head swung round unwillingly from the ordered patterns in front of him.

'Changing the order of the cards, that's cheating.'

82

'Why?' Paul asked.

'You're obviously going to get all the cards down if you change the order of the pack. It's going to work out every time.'

'Yes.' Paul considered. 'Isn't that the point of the game?'

I looked at him and nodded weakly. 'Yes. I suppose it is.' I was rolling a cigarette and a silly laughter was on its way up. I liked these people.

I sensed that Cathy was looking at me. I acknowledged her pleasantly and regarded my tobacco. She let her knitting fall. I retreated. She was a mess of a girl, arrived from nowhere and left cautiously to herself by the others. There was something very depressing about her which she seemed to foster; she made occasional efforts to be gay but no one wanted to be drawn in. She was looked upon as a kind of casualty. Henri had dismissed her as a lazy slut when I made inquiries. We all had a habit of rescuing each other from her company. Luc occasionally took her up as a matter of conscience and talked to her earnestly, but he could only shrug when asked about her. No one knew exactly what she was doing here; they were confident that she would move on.

'But *isn't* it cheating?' She stared fixedly at me.

'Possibly . . . it could be . . . ' I searched for a match. Paul was the rescuer.

'It's stupid to say that there are rules. Especially when you're only playing with yourself.' He gathered the cards together and put them away over the fireplace. Cathy shook her head and adopted her knitting.

'*Bon.* What time is it?' I stood up.

'Half-past six,' Cathy read from her watch.

'What time shall we do the cows?' I was desperate to escape.

'We'll go at seven,' Voyou announced.

'Good, there's time to finish my book.' I walked heavily

out of the room, feeling her eyes on my back. The rain battered on the tin roof over the porch.

As I opened the door to the landing, Christine's voice died away and the corridor was silent. I lay on my bed, wondering restlessly what might be happening in her room. I was claimed by the familiarity of page 117, but page 118 was too much; I decided that I'd have to start the book again in order to do it justice. I chose the year 1992; that might be a safely distant future for justice.

I lay and stared at the flies, listening to the snores from Pierre and the absolute silence from Luc and Christine. I heard Luc get up, walk past my room and go downstairs, leaving the door to swing shut behind him.

There was no view out of the window; the clouds had closed right in. I sprawled and stirred, and sprawled. I felt urgently close to Christine. I imagined her a lot of ways, mostly naked. It was a simple decision. Ten steps.

I found refuge in numbers; it might be twelve steps across to her bed.

'*On y va?*' Voyou interrupted, calling from downstairs.

I was fast off the bed. In half a second I had the door open, and I was frighted by the shock of immediate someone else. Christine let out a short scream; one hand on her heart, the other rushed to her mouth. She was just at my door in her bare feet.

We laughed at our fright, and stood absurdly; her eyes looked everywhere for an untrue explanation.

'The cows . . . ' I suggested, and I went away down the corridor, already exasperated at not having reached for her. The violence of this cowardliness; I felt it rebounding against myself as I searched anxiously through the waterproofs hanging in the porch. Voyou's cheery remarks jittered. I searched through the whole rack without recognising why I was looking or what I was looking for. Voyou waited, stamping his feet; one hand on the churn. I looked at him for guidance. He *was* extraordinary; clad

84

from chin to ankles in a vast, buttoned, army mackintosh. He might have been some weird *haute couture* creation, had it not been for the toothless grin and the mop of split, curly hair.

'*Tu es malade, ou quoi?*' The damp figure spoke, too.

'*Rien.* It's nothing.' I laughed and pulled out an anorak. We set off, up towards the farm, the churn banging against our calves as we slipped in the mud.

It was bleak. It was a different world. The poultry were a mess. The ducks were happy enough, but the chickens didn't appear for the evening grain. The cock gargled dismally from the deserted dunghill, wary as his own sound was thrown back upon him by the close-fitting atmosphere. The paranoid brothers hobbled up in a mud-bespattered file.

Napoleon felt that the onus was on him to raise his crest and take charge of their defence against the humans. A safe yard off the end of Voyou's boot, he hissed his orders to nobody but the miserable turkey, who hopped once and gave up; a cringing, tawdry, sodden ragbag.

But I was still racing through the moments in the corridor, reconstructing every minute of my flight, wondering what Christine was doing now, replaying it and winding it back until it lost its outline and was exhausted. It was filled only with an oppressive gloom that mirrored the drizzle.

I nudged the flank of the large amber cow. Memé's heavy bulk jerked up off the floor. She turned to survey me, strings of green dribble hanging from her mouth. She swallowed and stood solemnly, regurgitating and swinging her bottom jaw. She was a dream. She was our cow. The others came up from the valley for a summer feast; they were poisoned by the fluoride from the factory, they were dying slowly like the vines and the immigrant labour. The landowners kept these dreadful skeletons in slow decay so that they could claim compensation. Memé was part of an élite.

The other cow was a slattern, and perhaps the storm hadn't improved her temper. I started with her. It was a constant battle. She shifted and kicked out nervously. Twice the bucket was tipped over before I could anticipate her movements. And she whisked her tail round, swiping me across the cheek, smearing my face with her dung.

I leaned back on the stool and wiped my face dry. The great mass of brown and white stood planted firmly. Perhaps she had settled. I bent forward and under her; and she kicked for my elbow. I was quickly out of the way.

Voyou came squelching through the mud and the door creaked open. He, too, was at the end of his temper; his face khaki with dung, eyes smouldering.

'*Ça marche pas?*'

'No.'

'It's the storm.' He reached forward for the udders. The cow moved off to one side and raised a foot in warning. Voyou grabbed a plank and whacked her hard on the haunches. He hit her again, then a third time across the knees. She was still. He patted her and he milked her quickly.

There was no such trouble with Memé. I had my forehead close in on her big, warm flank; the milk spurted on to the mousse inside the bucket. I heard the gulping of her stomachs and the soft pause before she fell into her own monotonous rumination. It calmed me. There had been a lot of electricity in the atmosphere one way and another. I felt tired. It wouldn't happen again; or if it did, it would happen peacefully. Christine and I would not be so skittish with each other. But it wouldn't happen. That opportunity had been something stolen out of the vibrancy of the evening; it was a final bolt for a closing door.

The milk filtered through into the churn. Voyou was in a hurry to be finished for the night. He stood with his two cows, waiting to take them up to the pasture. I slammed the top on the churn, washed the filter under the tap and went back into the stable. I reached under Memé's neck and let the heavy chain drop down to the floor. Memé wheeled and looked mournfully at the weather. I slapped her out and the other cow followed her lead. They knew the routine so well that it was almost unnecessary to accompany them along the road. I always did; it was pleasing to lean on a stick and amble along behind the cows as they trudged off towards their food.

The mist was all around us. You could see only fifty yards. The drizzle had become a sort of clinging gas. We walked in silence, occasionally reaching out with the stick to keep the cows moving. One of the farm dogs joined us, coat oily with rain; it panted gushes of steam.

I huddled into the anorak; Voyou was lost in thought. We arrived at the pasture and closed the gate behind us. The cows stood drearily, watching us leave. Three hours ago it had been high summer and now it was autumn.

'I like the mountains; I like the way the weather changes. It's never the same.' Voyou relapsed into silence. There would be no scything tomorrow. I looked across at him. It was as if Voyou had shrugged off a deep self-discipline and was recognising that familiar part of himself which he had shelved during the rush of summer.

'What do you do in winter?' I asked.

'Sleep and have children,' Voyou decided.

'Yes?'

'Yes.' The grin was back; Voyou was pleased with himself. We came down to the farm and collected the churn.

'Is Frédérique pregnant?' I smiled.

'Yes.' He was shy with the news.

'Congratulations.' I shook his hand. Voyou's eyes beamed.

'It's not difficult.' He smeared the shit across his face

87

with a careless brush of his sopping coat-sleeve. 'It's very easy. Tac-a-tac tac, hup; like the goats.'

'Yes, but it's a decision,' I said paternally.

'Pfff . . . ' Voyou waved it aside.

'It'll change things a bit, being a father.'

'It's an evolution, that's very important.' He dumped the churn down in the mud, staring at my reaction. 'It's the evolution which is important, we can't stay the same. Who knows what will happen? I don't know. We'll see.'

'But you're pleased.'

'Yes.' He avowed.

'And the others?'

'They'll hear about it.' Voyou laughed. He half extended a hand. 'It's not serious, *mon brave*. We will evolve without intellectual decisions.'

'I was only thinking of space.'

Voyou shrugged. We picked up the churn again, suddenly keen to be back inside the house.

'Then we will evolve into a village. We will have another house, two or three houses; we'll build a village. If we have to buy it then we will work for the money. It *will* come, believe me. Anarchy. If you take it. If you don't take it, and you don't take responsibility for it, then you don't deserve it. That is very important.' Once again Voyou was adamant; the churn rested on the ground.

'Yes.' I tapped my fingers on the cold aluminium. Voyou grunted his approval. We moved forward in silence, pausing only by the porch to collect the bottles which the villagers left to be filled with milk.

'That's not the way it is in England?' Voyou asked.

'I don't know. It's not so . . . ' I couldn't find any word.

'*Engagé*, perhaps. Plenty of discussion about fair play . . . ' Voyou was scornful, shaking his head bitterly. 'That is very civilised. And then when the people are asleep with the boredom of listening, the bourgeoisie do what they want. *Non?* That's honest.' He laughed. 'I take what I want, my friend, it's best to leave the fair play to the toad on the Cross.'

We had a small candle-lit dinner, six of us. The others had all gone to bed. The evening crumbled away before the weather. It was understood that the scythers would lie in late and that the girls would do the milking.

As if to rub in his point, Voyou won another two games of backgammon. I went up to bed, leaving only Cathy downstairs by the stove. In one fell swoop, the mood of the place had utterly changed, and people had shut themselves away in reserve. I went on to page 119 and left the book on the pillow beside me.

It was a lethargic morning. Everyone must have done the same as I did, peering out from under the blankets at the white sauce of mist or cloud which clung to the window. Breakfast dragged through until eleven o'clock; people arrived with their sleep, puffy-eyed and disjointed, shutting the door behind them quickly and hugging themselves to keep the cosiness of the bed intact. There was a fortnight's worth of slumber encroaching from behind dulled eyes. It was a comparatively minimal task but no one could be bothered to go up the mountain to fix the cable and send the hay on down. It would stay under the tarpaulin until the sun shone again.

We littered the kitchen. If someone left for a moment, it was the signal for three or four to stand up and stretch, pick up a book or a pack of tobacco, make coffee, collect weaving, check the accounts, and sit down again in different seats. The dogs got tired of being trodden on. Marc and Paul drifted into preparing lunch, Christine bit her nails. I smiled at her and she looked away angrily. The day was over before it had begun.

In the evening, I went out to scythe grass for the rabbits and was lost to the world within a hundred yards. The mist shut everything down. The world was noiseless. The mountain, the farm and the whole spirit of the commune became intangible as it retired from this blank, clammy shroud. Everyone looked up when I came back in. For the first time there was food left on the table at the end of supper and no one bothered the cats as they picked their way over the plates.

The electricity arrived without comment. It was a night for leaving laundry in soak and going to bed.

I was surprised at the hold the weather had taken. Luc wasn't interested. The weather was there. Not to be ignored. There was a chapel further up the mountain. It had been built by the villagers after an avalanche had stopped thirty metres above the first house. The weather had its say. It was three days until the next full moon. The weather would change. Time for bed.

We had ourselves adapted the next day, and in the afternoon we formed up for an attack on the firewood needed for winter.

'*Bon. Assez.*' Voyou at an early breakfast enrolled Henri's manic inaction. 'We'll need at least four for the forest.' Nods all round the table. 'We'll go after lunch.'

I took myself off to clean out the pigsty. The sow was still young enough to take care of herself so the job was a pleasure. She was reserved and embarrassed at catching my eye; and unashamedly moody, grabbing the pitchfork when I left it resting against the wall and chewing it in outrage. Then she wasn't keen on me moving her trough, so she planted both feet firmly into her food until I pushed her away. She shook her jowls from side to side and rubbed along the walls, skidding on the wet floor and grunting in complaint. I talked to her; it was a relief to talk English to somebody, a double favour when she allowed me some personal speculation over and above guessing the weight of the next bale. I was so involved with her that I failed to notice Christine, watching me from the doorway, covering her nose in disgust. And when I did notice, Christine turned on her heel and went out.

Jewels

I gave the last barrowful of sludge to the delighted hens; I scattered sawdust and fresh straw over the sow and her domain. She snouted round in blessed exuberance, jerking her front legs off the ground and standing stockstill to peer at me from under an askew crown of stalks. Then she was hectic again, burrowing and snouting wildly.

I caught up with Christine as she came out of the henhouse with a clutch of eggs resting in her sweater.

'*Bonjour, m'sieur.*' She curtsyed sarcastically, bristling with resentment. I offered to take some of the eggs from her but she refused.

'Do you think we should talk?' I asked.

'No. You can talk to the pig. Why do you talk to the pig?' she demanded. 'It's stupid.'

'Because the pig talks English.' I stuck up for it.

'Yes?' She didn't want to smile.

'Christine?' She looked at me and looked away. Her eyes were hunted. 'So that's enough, is it?'

'Yes. If you wish.' She kept her eyes on the path.

'You don't think it's difficult?'

'What is? What is difficult?' she asked innocently. She was in control; she was pleased. She looked again at me, her eyes were ugly with greed. She cast them down, as if she recognised that they were not her best asset. She gave me some of the eggs to carry.

'Do you like dancing?' she asked, pensively.

'Yes.' I latched on to it.

'I like dancing. And Voyou likes to dance. We'll have a fire tonight and drink a lot of wine and dance. We'll have a party against the rain. If the others don't want to dance, too bad. *Je t'aime bien.*'

'And then we'll make love.'

'Ah oui . . . ' she trilled, childishly, in a voice that exasperated so much. It was a remnant of her unpractised appeal to men; now a grotesque cosmetic of innocence. It

91

laid a hundred false scents. It wasn't at all captivating. I watched her wearily. She sang her way down the hill, calling for me to follow her. Lunch was ready.

This first time, I didn't appreciate the beauty of the forest. We were soon all drenched from the moisture in the air and on the shrubs. I stood around helplessly, hating every minute of it – the dull, inanimate trees, the drab colourlessness of the forest floor, the feverish brute activity of the others and my own sweat that collected under the waterproof.

It would have been the best time to have opted for a siesta, back at the house; to have taken Christine. Perhaps the only available time. I didn't look what I was doing and the chopper bounced off the branch with a ring, missing my knee by a fraction. That was enough. To hell with her.

I laboured through it. We heaved the dead wood across a gully with picks and loaded it into the back of the truck. We jolted down the side of the ravine, over the rushing torrent and up the other side to the house, the dogs loping along beside us.

I went straight indoors while they unloaded the wood. I wanted only to take a warm shower and get cleaned up. I sat over a coffee and gloomily regarded the blackboard – I had marked myself down to milk the goats with Françoise, in an effort to get to know her.

Pierre came in and sat on the bench. We agreed that the forest was exhausting. It was a preliminary remark. The room was empty but for the two of us.

'I want to do the milking with Françoise; will you change?' Pierre asked. 'I'm down for the garden.'

'Sure.'

'I want to talk to her. Sometimes it's difficult. But with the milking there are only two of you; it's intimate.' Pierre dunked his bread and jam in hot milk. 'You know what I mean?'

'It's fine by me.'

'That's good then. You usually do it with Christine. She milks very fast.' Pierre seemed intent on his bread. I looked at him.

'Yes, she does.'

'We would like you to stay here,' Pierre announced. 'So there is money in the drawer if you want to buy a woman in the town.'

'How much?' I asked.

'Not much, but enough. We would like you to know. Perhaps it is not so important for you. You must take what you want.'

'Thank you.'

Pierre smiled. Who is we? I wondered. There were a lot of people whom I didn't know at all beyond a greeting and a banter; people with whom I had never milked and hardly ever talked. These people who suddenly came in from the periphery, or who started moving when I had them still.

'The language is sometimes difficult,' I murmured aloud.

'That is not important,' Pierre said, 'often we talk only about work. We are not intellectuals. You have the right spirit, we can see that. Perhaps more than Christine or Luc.'

'Different maybe. But right? They work as hard as anyone.' Christine pushed herself harder than most, and Luc got a lot done in his own way.

'It's not a question of work. You can do what you like. We don't care if you spend half the day being an artist . . . Work is not important; sacrificing yourself to the economy is not relevant. If you want to draw then you should draw. You shouldn't take what is here as the accepted way of life.'

'I am doing what I want,' I replied.

'If you are, that's good. There are a lot of people who

come here and work only to forget where they come from. They have to change because they give nothing but their work. They decide to leave. They don't realise that although there are no bosses here, each person must be his or her own boss, otherwise we are faced with the problem of servants . . . ' Pierre proceeded slowly, he didn't have his concepts off pat, like a pamphlet. He chiselled them out for his own consideration, emerging more surely with each stroke; the 'we' being the finest instrument of his craftsmanship, sometimes the hammer, at others the most delicate of points. His fingers tapped the table lightly when he searched for a word, his manner was always deferential to the idea in progress. He was concise and certain. When he came to the end, he stopped. He had been the first person who had taken the trouble to speak slowly and make sure that I had understood.

'You were a painter?' I asked.

'Yes.'

'But you don't paint here?'

'I stopped painting before I came here. I didn't like the Art people. Something was killing me. It's a very little flame which they want to make flare up and burn out so that they can go on without worrying too much. Capitalists must make use of everything, and as everything is running out they must make use of Art. I felt a danger that I would paint only my own ashes; or else I would waste my time painting theirs. You understand? I think you do. Otherwise you would not have stayed here.'

He drummed his callouses on the table. We were silent again. I looked at the blackboard.

'What about the garden?' I raised an eyebrow. 'What should I do in the garden?'

'Well,' Pierre considered, 'it's a bit boring. You have to unwind the hose and stand there for an hour watering the vegetables.'

94

'Right. I'll get it done now.'

I hauled myself off the bench, pulling my coat closer around me, thinking about Pierre and 'we'. I didn't need the money for a whore.

Pierre came with me to the door, going for the milk churn. I was first outside, zipping the coat against the cold.

'It's been raining for two days, should I just . . . ?'

Pierre was quietly tapping his finger on the side of his head.

I stepped out of the shower just as Voyou came through the back door with a half-dozen bottles of wine. He hailed my steaming nakedness, showing me off to Frédérique. She smiled slyly.

'At least you've got some muscle; not as intelligent as me yet . . . ' Voyou was exultant.

'But more beautiful,' Frédérique pushed him towards the kitchen, 'and a lot better smelling.'

'I smell of the land and the forest, open spaces . . . '

'And shit. Don't you want to take a shower? My darling . . . '

'Ho! Tonight – tac-a-tac tac tac tac. Heh?' Voyou laughed.

'He'll be too drunk,' Frédérique confided.

'Congratulations.' I stood with the towel. She looked surprised. Voyou nudged her belly with a wine-bottle. She blushed.

'Oh that one . . . '

'The little one.' Voyou dumped the wine-bottles on the floor and pulled her towards the shower.

'Show him. Show him the kid.'

'There's nothing to see yet, you fool.' She slapped his hands away.

'Of course there is. Look how beautiful and plump she's getting. What beautiful breasts.' He squeezed them

95

lovingly. She forced his head under the sweater, and raised her eyebrows in mock supplication.

'All right then, a shower!' she cried, suddenly shedding her self-consciousness with the sweater and pushing him under the hot water; smothering his laughter with her breasts. She was glorious as the water bedraggled them both.

'And soap!' She pushed it down his trousers.

'This is a terrible woman,' Voyou howled. 'God save us from women . . . '

'And from men who take what they want.' With her head on one side, her hair dangling away from her cheek, she slowly emptied a bottle of shampoo over him, the water streaming down her skin and filling her rubber boots. 'You may now kiss me. And I hope you did the washing today, otherwise we'll be walking round naked tomorrow.'

'Then tomorrow we'll stay in bed until these clothes dry. *Bon.*' Voyou rubbed his hands.

I slipped away. I took the wine into the kitchen, to where the pressure cooker sizzled grandly and thick yards of wood crackled in the fireplace, watched by Luc. He lifted his eyes curiously as I came into the room.

The others were all busy. Henri clattered through the lunchtime washing-up, Belline sniffed a sauce and Marc was wiping down the long trestle table. The milkers were still confined in the mist. I poured the first glasses of wine and sat by the chimney, drying my hair, listening to Winifred Atwell.

Luc brooded. He took the guitar off the wall and picked at the strings, discarding several half-attempted tunes. He got bored. He stretched his arms along the back of the bench, swung his feet up on to a small table and appeared to doze.

The door opened softly. I felt the draught and looked up. Christine walked across the room, poured herself a glass of wine and sat within easy reach of Luc. He didn't welcome her. He cast an eye over her and looked back at the fire. She had got herself dressed up; a black cotton shirt with a low neckline, and she had made up her eyes. She regarded the distance between them and sang soundlessly to herself, along with the music, draining the wine in three gulps, then looking down at the floor and picking at her fingers.

The record ended. She went over to change it. She chose a collection of old French pop songs. Luc tapped his boots together, vaguely in time to the music, more of a gesture than an involuntary enjoyment. The music became mawkish and syrupy, one of those dreary Continental songs; all the emotion cranked up repetitively and all life squeezed out of it at the second stanza. They hadn't a very good collection of records. The collecting had stopped dead when they arrived at the mountain.

Luc shifted restlessly. She tried to talk to him, he gave her a phlegmatic grunt. I felt sorry for her, confronted by this stolid indifference when she was searching to create a party spirit.

Luc clumped to the other side of the room, searching for something to do. Henri was across from the sink in a flash, wiping his hands on his trousers, skimming the needle off the record, muttering to himself. He put on the other side of the Winifred Atwell, and brushed past Christine.

'Bloody pop music. Drives you insane. Wanking. Like a bloody funeral.' He knelt quickly in front of me, poking his cigarette into the edge of the fire; retrieving it and puffing on it, a few quick draws.

'Oh, I like it. But I like this one too.' Cathy came eagerly out of the shadows to talk.

'Hm . . . ' Henri was up; dismissive but a little uncertain. 'It's all the same anyway. Consumer junk.' He picked up the hairbrush, which we all used apart from Christine, and gave his hair a careless, efficient flattening. He squeezed cautiously at his face in front of the mirror; he hadn't a good complexion. Always under the truck, or talking to himself and his tools in the workshop, grinning affectionately when they cut him, he expressed himself only through his hands and agreed brusquely whenever he was spoken to. Hanging on the edge of any discussion, he felt the weight of his incoherence keenly and hated the pressure put on him by calm intellectual cleverness. He would occasionally tell stories of his army days, which amused him enormously by their wastage and bumbling. He ignored visitors in a studious way, loved accidental clowns and story-tellers, and became intensely irritable with anyone who sat down for more than ten minutes at a time during the day. Bed was with the alarm clock and Françoise, if she wasn't sleeping with Pierre. He always laughed eagerly, as if he thought that the reserve of laughter in the world might evaporate and he wanted his share.

Christine stuck her tongue out at him. Without Luc's support and with her inability to turn the head of this workman, she was downcast. Her face was ugly and spoiled. She sulked.

With the arrival of Voyou, clean and playful, she brightened up. Voyou came to the party in the only clothes left to him; his red and black patterned pyjamas and his farm boots. He turned all the music off and sang a short nonsense song, accompanying himself on the guitar. There was applause.

'Bon, eh?' Voyou was delighted.

When the farm was begun, everybody threw in whatever money they could get their hands on. It wasn't more than a thousand pounds. Voyou had three francs, a hammer and a dozen chickens which had fallen off the back of a lorry. And now he was the emperor, striding round the kitchen to wolf-whistles while Frédérique laughed at him from the door.

The milkers returned and were ordered to wash off the stains of their work-lined day – Voyou refused to dance with any stinking peasants – and Luc was finally obliged to emerge from his mood. The cats and dogs were thrown outside to find their own festivity. A feast was assembled, joined by a serving dish of duck and cemented by a babble of chatter.

Three descending shepherds called in and were invited to stay. There was another crate of booze.

Two hours later we were flushed with the wine, the windows were thrown open and the dancing commenced with Voyou's weaving turkey-shuffle to 'The Pipes of Pan'. None of the women could match him. It was the men, roaring drunk and making fools of ourselves, who hopped round the floor in tight short steps, occasionally reeling off-balance and pushed back into the mêlée by the laughing girls. And when the men capsized, looking for more wine, Pierre called Françoise, Annie and Belline to show their colours in a Breton dance – the shepherds raucous in their admiration, the girls tossing their hair disdainfully, Voyou taking up the challenge; we swirled clumsily in the hot kitchen, banging our heels down on the planks. There was suddenly an accordion as Polaud arrived from the village with a bottle, and now everyone was on the floor, feeding each other from waist to waist, flirting madly, hands everywhere, caught up in the joy of prolonging the riot for ever.

More cautious knocks on the door that nobody heard, and there were the three old widows, standing back against the wall, smiling and chattering and pointing, being prevailed upon to dance and refusing, so embarrassed and yet blessing the surge of life on their mountain, which had been left for dead and had then been challenged by these mad people who danced in that wild way that comes only from pride.

'It is like this in England?' One of them looked down at me – bent double, taking a breather.

'Yes . . . sometimes . . .' I couldn't explain over the din, nor did I want to. And what could I describe? The mattresses against the wall, lined with drugged apathetics; the lifeless, sexy movements of prematurely geriatric careerists; the spastic jerking of nihilists; the posed contortions of the narcissistic.

'Yes . . .' I smiled at her old, lined face.

'Ah, it is good over there. I have heard.' She was pleased for me. 'You will not stay here for long. The life is too hard.'

'No . . .' I grinned at her. I asked her to dance again. She refused. I protested. She shook her head and waved me away, back into the throng. Frédérique grabbed me to her, put her arms round my neck, whispered hotly how drunk she was. I hugged her tight and we were pushed along by the jostle, lost in it. She had a lovely body.

'Take me outside,' she mumbled.

I guided her through the shifting maze. I saw Christine, dancing with one of the shepherds, keeping him at arm's length; she was miserable, answering his lechery with her eyes on the floor. Luc was off with Françoise, guiding her steps with his strength, throwing her out and pulling her back to him again, teasing her with his effortless domination over her reels. Voyou was in the middle of a fervent discussion. Marc was drip-feeding Polaud with wine.

I reached the door and stumbled through it, suddenly the music was behind us and the clouds menaced with chill. Frédérique and I hugged, arms round each other.

'How do you feel?' I said.

'I thought I was going to faint,' she whispered. 'Just a minute or two more.'

'As long as you like.' But not really. Already she was under the shower again, the full breasts and the hair slipping away from the loving, almost pensive, face. She moved her knee back from my thigh.

'Ah, thank you.' She rubbed her face and yawned, disengaging herself. She stepped backwards, almost falling. I reached her. 'I'm going to sit on the step for a moment.'

'Don't fall asleep,' I warned against the cold. The mist pushed right in under the porch roof. It was quiet. I wanted to get back inside.

'Two minutes. No. I feel better.' Brushing back her hair, she stood up and opened the door.

The widows were interested; the party would last a week for them, every little piece of observation about the couples would be dissected with a shaking of heads and an excited speculation.

Polaud was in his cups and describing miraculous wild boars to a sceptical Marc and an open-mouthed Henri. The shepherds forecast the end of the bad weather. The others stood on the dance-floor, caught by the sudden ending of the music, wanting to continue.

Christine was at the record-player, looking through the records until she found the rock and roll she wanted. I drank a glass of water, killing time in the corner until the music was loud and I could take her when she returned to the fray. She chose the affable old English monkey, his sneer starting across the room and Charlie Watts stamping in behind him. I knew this song from a number of mattresses, Christine from the night-clubs. It was a favourite of hers; she adored Mick Jagger. She looked for the room's approval. She dallied, putting a record back in its cover and arranging it.

I set off. The dancers were fewer in number and were more attached to strings. It was the kind of worldly music that made everyone subservient. They performed to each other.

I was half-way round the side when I was snatched and

lurched against and hauled into the circle by Cathy. She was not to be avoided. She was utterly drunk and I was not drunk enough to be able to push her away honestly. I tried a quick shuffle, guiding us towards Christine, but Cathy grabbed my arms.

'There's no need to be shy. You're always so shy,' she leered, in what she imagined to be encouraging sympathy. Fucking hell, I prayed, with luck she'll trip and fall into the fire.

We waltzed round the room; I stiff with horror, she all crutch and leg, her head flopping from side to side. Luc looked up approvingly at this happy occurrence; the two outsiders coming together. Voyou was splitting his sides with laughter. I pleaded with Paul, and he pretended not to notice.

Cathy searched for my neck with her lips. This was going to be a disaster. I managed to get hold of Pierre and Belline and form into a sociable knees-up. Thank God we managed to collect people; and when the record ended I got myself lost in the confusion of detachment.

That was it for the canned music. We'd had enough of being trough-fed. I lost sight of Christine. Polaud's voice was rising in an epic tale of the *dahu*, that mystical mountain beast which had its left legs a foot shorter than its right legs and which ran at incredible speed in an anti-clockwise direction round and round the mountain, seemingly immune to bullets and too fast for dogs. Henri was impressed.

'But *I* caught it.' Polaud eased the cap off his head and scratched. Henri and he were so drunk that they swayed from side to side in unison. '*I* caught it.'

Henri considered the I, the catching, and the it.

'How?' He focused somehow on the question.

'I hid behind a bush, and when it came, *mon brave*,' Polaud slapped Henri on the shoulder, dropping his voice to a confidential shout: 'and when it came, I leapt out of the bush and scared it so much with this face of mine that it turned round and rolled down the hill.'

The laughter was suppressed in everyone. Henri was better sport than the story. Henri paused. The onus was on him. He swayed and succeeded in keeping his eyes open.

'Why did it fall down the hill?' he managed to ask, out of his perplexity.

'Because when it turned round, its short legs were downhill and its long legs were uphill. So it overbalanced.'

There was a thunderclap of laughter all around the room at the hapless Henri, who grinned stupidly beside Polaud's sparkling eyes. He still wasn't sure what was happening. He let himself be led away. As they opened the door, Christine came back in – the men all looked at her.

'And that is why you always have to chase a *dahu* in a clockwise direction.' One of the shepherds, a little old man of fifty, stood up with the intention of leaving; he hitched up his trousers, and was chastised by his juniors.

'Ho! Where are you going?'

'Sit and drink!'

'We're well enough here. The bars are closed.'

'The women are beautiful.'

'You don't know when you're well off.'

'Sit and drink.'

'And the sheep?' he expostulated.

'Tomorrow.'

'They're still there.'

The little fellow shook his head. 'I go up the mountain now or I don't go at all.'

'We don't go at all. That's easy.'

'Ringo! Caesar!' The dogs were at his feet in an instant. 'There's fog; we go back now.'

The two youngsters grumbled to their feet.

'Ah, you never get sick of fucking sheep, Marcel,'

Polaud hollered obscenely.

'If I had a wife like yours, I'd take a sheep every time,' came the riposte.

'If you had a wife like mine, you'd take anything; even my wife!' Polaud laughed. Christine clucked her tongue, pouted, and giggled. The other girls were hostile to the bawdiness.

'Christine, Christine; come home with me, Christine!' Polaud impored her.

'*Oh là là . . .*' Christine revelled in the attention.

'Take her.' Luc waved his hand. He was very drunk.

'With us, Christine; you don't want an old man like that!' the shepherds joked.

'Come on, Polaud,' said the old fellow, 'we'll give you a ride in the jeep.'

'There's good wine at home,' Polaud shouted.

'We'll drink it then.'

They moved to the door with their farewells and gratitude, falling down the steps. There was a brief skirmish between the various dogs and the thump of a boot into fur.

'Away, away . . .' and a song took up their four voices until they were lost in the mist.

'You know how old he is?' Marc was at my elbow. I took my eyes off Christine.

'Who?'

'The old fellow.'

'Fifty, fifty-five?'

'Thirty-two.'

'*Non!*' I shook my head.

'*Oui!* Luc! How old is Marcel?'

'Thirty-two.' Luc was chucking Christine under the chin, teasing the pretty little object. Marc was victorious.

'It's the mountains.'

'And the drink,' Belline put in.

'But you notice how there are always old women and

104

hardly ever old men.' Marc made his point.

Paul was at the cards, sweeping plates and glasses away down the table with his arm. Annie gently took them from him and invited him to bed. His head sank in agreement, burying itself against her thighs until he found the energy to climb the stairs.

Voyou had the guitar, cradling it seriously. He started on a song. '*Non.*' He broke off and tried again. 'That one?' He was the least drunk of them all.

'I'm going to bed.' Marc went up with Belline. There were only Luc, Pierre and Christine left at the party. We pulled chairs round the fire and settled with the last bottle. Luc was mumbling at Christine, staring into the flames. Her eyes darted over the room. He was being serious about something, and she provided the necessary attention. It was going in one ear and out of the other. It wasn't in her nature to learn, but she set herself to seem as if she were trying.

'Don't play a song, Voyou,' Pierre suggested, 'just play.'

'Ah, those days are gone.' Voyou shook his head and took some tobacco in his hand, bending over it. 'We're going to have a baby in the house. Frédérique's pregnant.' He looked up with his grin.

'Good,' Pierre said simply.

Christine was too overjoyed. It betrayed a mixture of envy and disgust.

Luc looked into Voyou's eyes like an interested patriarch.

'*Bon.*' Voyou applied himself to the guitar. He tinkered for a few seconds, and the tinkering was hanging there again some twenty minutes later when he put the guitar down. There was unspoken approval and contentment. Pierre was asleep. Voyou shook him; he wouldn't wake up. I hadn't the impulse to move.

'It'll be warm enough down here,' Luc grunted.

'And there are blankets.' Christine knew how to arrange.

'Call me early; about noon,' Voyou suggested, closing the door behind him.

'We'll probably see him in a minute when he finds she's been sick on his pillow again.'

Luc was irritable. Christine jumped at the chance to please him.

'Who wants some mint tea?'

I raised my hand feebly. She went down the room collecting cups, and she shut the windows. A heavy silence settled. She opened the door to a whining dog. It sniffed at the various sets of boots and finally chose to flop down with its chin on its paws at Pierre's feet. I watched it rather than look at Luc.

The water boiled in the saucepan and three glasses of tea appeared on the table. Christine and I sipped immediately; Luc left his to get cold, as an insult to her.

'Strange thing, love,' Luc muttered. 'You fall into bed in circumstances which collect out of nowhere and then everyone's in couples and the children start dropping round your neck.'

'But Voyou's pleased?' Christine complained half-heartedly, anxious to gauge the depth of his mood.

'Yes. She's lucky. That's the one thing she couldn't plan out in her head.'

'Well he is pleased and he sees it as an evolution,' I snapped. Christine bit her nails and stayed out of it.

'Anything's an evolution,' Luc grunted scornfully. 'What is evolution; anything that happens?'

'The farm is strong enough to be able to cope with a baby, isn't it?'

'*Bien sûr*. It's not the babies, it's the couples.'

'It takes two to make a baby,' I said. Christine giggled. 'It seems to have developed into couples; maybe that's natural.'

'I don't think it need be natural, and it's certainly not

evolution. Françoise has Pierre and Henri. All three of them are happy, and they're not closed off.'

Christine gulped at her tea. Luc went on.

'It's the slow closing-down into couples. That's not why we're here, that's not what I understand by the word communal. If a baby makes two people into more of a couple, then it's not a good thing. If all we get here is women feathering their nests . . . ' He shrugged disdainfully.

I couldn't speak for women. 'And Cathy?' I asked. Christine looked at me quickly. She sat demure next to Luc's long slump.

'Do you desire her?' Luc muttered.

'No. Do you?'

'No. No one does. She's a problem. She never makes an effort. Maybe she doesn't want to be desired.'

Christine snorted. Luc scowled at her.

'Not like Christine, dear little Christine. She wants to be desired, don't you?' He didn't bother to look at her. She froze; her eyes crawled along the floor. 'She tries, in her own way.' He patted her knee paternally.

'She succeeds; don't you like it?' I sneered.

Luc reached his massive hand up to squeeze her breast, to see how far he could humiliate her.

'Don't, Luc . . . ' she murmured, 'I don't like it when you're in this mood.'

She glanced spitefully at me. Luc kept his hand where it was, playing the cruel schoolboy. I stood up and stretched.

'Look at her; she's very desirable, this little Christine.'

I turned. Luc had wrenched the cotton shirt up over her breasts and the brassière with it. Her breasts clung to her, small and white against her tanned skin. Luc rubbed his heavy finger across the nipple and she was aroused, looking down at it childishly. It wasn't in spite of herself; she knew that I was also aroused. She looked at me.

107

'If you desire her, you should make love to her.' Luc
lost interest in the exhibition and leaned back on the
bench, yawning generously. She remained a moment the
way she was, then she let the cotton shirt fall back down to
her waist, covering her again.

'Very beautiful,' I said, 'thank you.' She blushed and
went back to the wine.

'Because that's another problem,' Luc droned on, 'and
it affects the commune. I was slow to see it until Christine
told me and asked me about the responsibility; how I felt,
what she should do . . . ' The confessor went on with his
lecture, warming to the position of power and responsibility.

'What a lot of wank . . . ' I thought suddenly; and I
pitied her. Her adolescence must have been a nightmare.
She sat, tired and cowed. There was nothing of this
between us; the passion which had existed was being
shackled to this vile mausoleum of liberal rationales.

'Good night,' I interrupted; 'sleep well.' She looked up
and smiled.

'You too,' she said blankly. She tried to be coquettish.
She was pale. She tried to make it attractive.

I marked myself down to milk the cows with Françoise,
and went upstairs.

I was on one leg, having difficulty with the second
boot, when the door opened and Cathy came in. I sighed,
but she didn't go away. She helped me undress. She
whispered continuously; such things as 'I was waiting for
you to come to bed' and 'I first wanted you when you
were sunbathing and I saw your sex moving inside your
pants'. I heard her, and I mumbled. She left me in my
shirt and took off her nightdress. She was ugly. She knelt
over me and gobbled. She had a lot of grunting to get rid
of. I helped myself. She got up when we had finished,
early in the morning. We didn't bother each other.

It was possibly the communal hangover, and possibly the fourth day of the mist. It was one of those 'Why are we here?' days. We whipped ourselves vigorously.

It started because Henri had lit the wood-fired stove and Christine chose to heat up her coffee on the gas cooker. Henri flung in a remark about wastage. Christine ignored it, giving him the scornful look which implied that there might be finer things in life than half a centimetre of Calor Gas. Henri decided that we would get rid of all the Calor Gas in the autumn.

'*Oui?*' Christine sauntered away blithely.

Françoise, for lack of anything else to do, agreed with Henri and complained about the state of the garden, which was her principal interest. If we all worked for two hours a day on the garden, then we would never have to buy anything from the supermarket, we wouldn't need to sell as much cheese, we wouldn't need so many goats and we wouldn't waste so much time on the hay.

'So then we'd waste the time on the garden,' Voyou, reading the same old newspaper, concluded briskly.

Henri felt that these economic equations got nowhere. He opted for idealism and decided that we would get rid of the cars and the truck, which were wasteful and unecological, and we would use horses.

'We can never catch the bloody horse,' Paul pointed out, 'so we wouldn't go anywhere.'

'Exactly. There'd be less of this pissing about and less pollution by the mentality of the capitalists and fools in the valley.' Henri was convinced that we had a battle on our hands; there was a capitalist behind every tree.

'You came from the valley,' Paul observed.

'Exactly. That's why I know the danger of it, that kind of mentality. We are here for something different, and some of us are losing sight of it.'

There was a pause while people wondered if they were part of the 'some of us', and if they wanted to get into a discussion. I could see defences springing up in case it got personal.

'Perhaps it's true,' Luc offered; 'we have to decide what we are here for.' We expected some pronouncement, but there was none. It was part of Luc's habit to introduce the question and then to evade committing himself. He would step in at the end and mop up with his milky humanitarianism.

'We are here because we are here.' Voyou turned the page. He never liked these arguments.

'We are here to build something,' Annie suggested.

'We're here because we don't want to be down there; we don't want to be isolated and exploited,' came from Pierre.

'Well, for all the isolation and exploitation down there, they certainly live well. Marcel's brother has just bought a house; the factory pays his electricity, his coal, his insurance, his children's education . . .' Marc reeled it off.

'His brain . . .' Voyou's eyes flashed.

'And do you think you need a brain up here? How do we use our brains? What brain does it take to plant a carrot or carry the bloody hay or milk a goat?!' Marc was furious.

'You want to live down there, you go and do it.' Voyou paid no attention. 'For me, I don't fit in that easily.'

'That's it. Exactly.' Henri lit his cigarette, excited. 'We don't fit in. If we weren't here, what else could we do? Nothing! That's why we have to cut ourselves off and make ourselves strong. We have nowhere else to go.'

'You speak for yourself; not for me. I'm not here out of despair.' Marc refused it.

'Me neither. I'm here because I believe in it.' Pierre joined forces. Marc went further into Henri.

'What you're saying is pure factory mentality; it's the kind of defeated mentality of only being here to work. It's

110

a mentality you've brought up here with you; if you're going to talk about pollution, then your attitude is no better than Christine using the Calor Gas. It's revisionist.'

'But . . . '

'There's no way you can get away from revisionism unless you keep running. And if you run, you create nothing.' Voyou had reached the sports pages. There was another pause. The women were suppressing their anger; the men ignored them as long as they could. It broke. There was a mêlée of argument, peculiarly mediaeval. There was no strategy. Sides were changed at the doff of a hat or a minor flattery.

The noise swept from one end of the room to the other, and back again. It erupted in small, fluid patches. And it ended with Luc earnestly describing the endeavour of his friend who had chosen to live apart from society in an underground burrow in the forest, living off berries and the bark from trees. Against such purism there was no rebuke. People were silent with respect. Henri looked as if he was about to hike out and try it.

I felt something hysterical welling up inside me. Pierre and I gushed with laughter at the same time, slapping each other on the shoulders. The others were dismayed. I couldn't explain. We went into a quick comedy act.

'*Bonjour.*'

'*Bonjour.*'

'*Ça va?*'

'*Ça va.*'

'How are you living?'

'I live in an anarchist commune of one.'

'Why is that?'

'Because all the decisions are unanimous.'

'And what have you decided?'

'To disappear up my own arsehole.'

There were polite smiles. Paul laughed; Cathy laughed longer. Voyou grinned and went to look out of the window. The mist was beginning to break up. We could see the roofs of the village further down and sometimes across to small patches of forest.

'What about it then?' Voyou asked. 'We need less theory and more wood.'

There were four of us not too hungover to go to the forest. I caught sight of the sun as we bounced down the road in the truck. We had to turn a hundred and sixty degrees on a sixpence – with a drop of several thousand feet – to get round the bend and on to the forest track. Voyou did it singing; it was that kind of exuberance at getting out of the kitchen.

We pulled up in the deep silence. It made you nervous and briskly self-assertive to be in front of these hundred-and-fifty-foot trees. We bustled around, collecting the two-handled saws, tucking choppers and ropes into our belts and taking an axe or a pick each.

It was a hard scrabble over the damp, rotten forest floor which slid away from the boot like sand; often necessary to grab the first bush or sapling to stop yourself from falling back. We climbed three hundred feet and stopped. It was like being at the bottom of the ocean. There was no breeze and no sound; the atmosphere was dense and cool, it was almost dark.

'What are we looking for?' I whispered.

'Number thirty-two,' came the short reply.

There were trees everywhere; what the hell was number thirty-two and what did it matter?'

'You look for a small patch, where the bark has been chipped off, and a number in red paint. Right; we spread out.' Voyou waved the posse away.

'How do we know it's here?' I asked.

'It's somewhere here.' Pierre was conspiratorial. We were tracking some revenge.

We fanned out, climbing sideways. Three minutes later, there was not a sound from the forest and I was on my own, except for the axe. I strained my ears, but there was nothing. The sky was only a small, light-blue counter, miles away. To look up, following the long, straight trunks, gave me the most intense vertigo.

I scrambled further. It was as quiet as the grave. I felt that I was committing sacrilege, creeping between the feet of these giants. I didn't dare look over my shoulder, even when I was breathless and my legs were stiff with pain. I put a hand against a trunk to haul myself up and it came away sticky with the tree's pungent-smelling blood. I couldn't wipe it off.

I sat on a rock, nervous. Giddy with the effort of climbing, it seemed that I was closing in on myself. There was no room here with the trees. The forest floor was dead and whatever sunlight the trees were breathing was too high up for me to reach. This was not a place where I could survive. There wasn't another hundred and forty-five feet in my species – however much perfection we all put into it – not now, nor in however many decades these trees would live. It was a gloomy thought. No; not gloomy. Not gloomy at all. Inevitable. No question of challenge. Somewhere in here there was a tiny white patch with a red painted number on it.

'Ho-ah-ho-ah-ho-ah-ho . . . '

There was the cry of the executioner. I started back towards the centre.

'Ho-ah-ho-ah-ho . . . ' the cry drew me closer.

They were all there before me. Voyou and Marc rocking backwards and forwards with the two-handled saw biting into the uphill side of the trunk, small particles of sawdust thickening the air and two piles of heavier offal trickling down the slope away from the stricken pine. Pierre leant against its neighbour.

They got as far as they could before the tree shifted imperceptibly and tried to rest back on the blade. Voyou and Marc worked it clear and stood to one side, exhausted.

'*Bon.*' Pierre spat on his hands. I picked up an axe and we swung alternately from down below, carving a wide vee into the fresh white wood; chips of flesh leaping into the air. We went at it for five minutes and I slowed. We lost the rhythm. Voyou took over. The tempo increased, sweat pouring from them both.

'*Attend!*' Marc kept his eyes on the top of the tree. '*Un petit moment . . .*'

We paused to calculate our escape route; where the tree would fall, how it might bounce; whether it would turn and where we should run to shelter from its throes. It would do us no good if we all leapt the same way and collided; the tree wouldn't wait for us to pick ourselves up and get out of the way. We were curiously confined in the centre of the forest.

I was assigned a spot off to the right. Marc and I were to finish it off; Voyou was to go the same way as me, and Pierre to the other side.

Voyou took himself and the ropes out of reach. Pierre picked up the saw and leant against the same tree as before, breathing deeply. Marc spoke.

'O.K.?'

'O.K.'

'As soon as it starts moving, leave it. Don't run, but move quickly. We can always come back if it decides only to flirt with us.'

I nodded.

We started again. The axes thudded in. We went slowly. A chip hit my cheek, causing me pain. I ignored it. It was difficult now to get the axe down inside the vee.

Thud. Thud. Thud. Thud.

We both felt that we were having no impact. We speeded up. The tree didn't move.

'*Ça va!*' Pierre shouted. It was a strange last thing ever to say, I thought later, after the shock.

'*Ça va!*'

114

I saw it. I turned and ran blindly. I lost the axe. I hesitated for it. I felt Voyou's hand on my shirt, pulling me out of the way. There was creaking. I stood and watched, with Voyou's hand still resting on my shoulder.

The great tree leaned. It twisted round, straining to leave its axis. It hung, like a massive wave, turning slightly towards us; it picked up speed from nowhere. Voyou dragged me back still further; the top was moving very fast.

'*Attention! Mal tombé!*' Voyou warned.

And as it came, the top of the tree slid down the trunk of another, to its left and over a drop. It was pinioned at its centre by a massive pine on the right. The top flopped down with a thunderous crack. The tension was too great; there was a silence which dragged. In terrible slow motion, our tree peeled itself away from its base, the huge trunk swung upwards into the air and moved slowly, waist-high, away from us and towards the trapped Pierre.

No one said anything. It wasn't up to us. It was inevitable. It was moving slowly but such a mass wouldn't stop at flesh and bones.

Pierre was curiously unconcerned. He was too exhausted. He was smiling hesitantly with his hand on the saw. I remembered that smile when I was in Oxford Street, crossing the road; when I was on a Channel ferry, and at other times. Voyou's fingers dug into my shoulder.

And then, for some reason known only to itself, the great tree stopped.

I brushed at a trickle of sweat on my temple. I felt weak, I felt Voyou's weakness beside me, his hand falling away from my shoulder. The silence of the forest jumped in.

'*Bon.*' Voyou pulled the chopper out of his belt and walked away. Pierre strolled down the other side of the tree, tapping his axe along the trunk.

I followed. It was decided to leave the top of the tree; it

wasn't worth the effort of pruning it. Voyou pushed one end of the saw into my hand. We knelt on opposite sides of the tree, not looking at each other. Marc and Pierre worked further up.

'I want a cigarette first.'

'We'll do this first,' Voyou stated flatly.

'You saw what I saw,' I challenged him.

'And what did you see?' Voyou kept his eyes on the bark, scratching the teeth of the saw across it.

'Pierre was nearly crushed.'

Voyou reflected, looking at his fingers.

'Or crippled.' Voyou looked up. His blue eyes were flat and dull. At the back of his mind he was dog-tired from the shock. He spoke in a long, semi-drunk litany; at times in anger.

'Listen to me. Only Pierre knows that. Next time he'll be more careful. There's a lot of danger, but he isn't hurt so there's no point in worrying about it. You have respect for the mountain. Then you forget and some day you learn again. *Bon*. Enough. We don't talk about it. It doesn't exist. Like a dream. Not worth talking about.'

He pushed the saw back over the trunk. We finished the cutting and Voyou was glad to get away and laugh with the others.

The tree was in three lengths and we went a little higher up for another one. It was quickly done; we had had our quota of danger for the day. We dug the picks into the wood and pulled it down to the waiting truck, hopping out of the way if the trunks took on too much speed and slid past us of their own accord. The forest floor was still wet. The last length went off like a torpedo, disappearing down the hill and crashing through the shrubs on a course of its own. We sent warning shouts after it.

'Bad luck for anyone at the bottom.' I was angry.

'Anyone who stands around at the bottom is an idiot,' Pierre said.

116

'Of course he is,' Voyou agreed. 'Have we got every-thing? Ropes?'

Ropes, picks, saws, axes. We went down the trail the trunk had smashed out for us. It was buried a foot deep in the road, about four metres from the truck.

'Good,' Voyou remarked, 'we won't have to go far to pick it up. Six lengths; that's enough planks for Henri's pottery roof.'

After coffee and a *tartine*, Marc and I went up to the pasture to collect the cows, which had been left to graze through the colder daytimes.

'I'll fetch them,' I offered.

'I'll keep you company; it's a beautiful evening.'

After all the rain, it wasn't warm; but the sun was dying in a cloudless, powder-blue sky and the air was charged with oxygen rather than dust. The clarity was remarkable. The forest had advanced almost to our doorstep, the great jawbone hanging above it. Behind us, you could see a long way across the mountain peaks. As we got to the farm, the chickens rushed out in a mob.

'False alarm . . . ' I laughed.

We ambled on up the road, hands in pockets. A neighbour looked over her fence and good-eveninged, dropping a remark about the weather. Further down the road, there was the hum of the cable as Henri, Paul and Luc sent the bales down to the barn.

I was standing by a concrete wall, looking up and smiling while Marc joked with the neighbour, and I suddenly knew that I was going to leave, while I still had the chance. I didn't ask myself why and I didn't dwell on the feeling. It wasn't even a decision. But tomorrow or the day after, in a week or a fortnight, I would leave.

I walked on slowly. I came to a bend in the road, where the pasture immediately dropped down towards the valley. The great jawbone reared above; there was an enormous mass of rock, tier upon tier of pointed crag, a glowing deep red in the sunset, magnificent. And beneath it – far beneath it; my eyes came down meekly and swam with the readjustment – there were the four tiny cows, plodding up through the green towards the gate, full bellies swinging and the sound of their bells tinkling over the air.

'*Beau, eh?*' Marc was smiling at my bewilderment. '*Oui, c'est beau.*'

'Yes.'

'Here, at this time, it is beautiful. Sometimes I stand here, completely mad with it. It gives tremendous hope, this beauty.'

'Yes.'

'You know; I think that one day I'll be standing here at this time and a little man will come down the road and his voice will say: 'Here, *mon vieux*, is the name of the hundred-to-one outsider that will win the Prix de l'Arc de Triomphe.'

We laughed; we walked on, waiting for the cows to reach the gate.

'And then what would you do with the money?' I asked.

'Nothing. But I would have won it. Without any sweat.'

'Pollution . . . ' I tutted.

'It's disgusting . . . ' Marc smiled.

It was back to the scything and the dawn. Another two weeks and it might be finished. I stayed, slowly easing myself away from involvement, catching odd people on their own and talking with them. It would be the best place in the world from which to watch the world die. The sun again blazed down on us and the bales thumped into the dust at the end of the cable.

I undertook one last enterprise. I collared Luc for an afternoon; we took a roll of barbed wire and twenty strong posts to build a pen outside, below the garden, for the sow. Everyone shook their heads and came to see the fun.

'She'll come out,' I assured them.

'Oh yes, she will,' Voyou laughed, 'and then you'll never see her again.'

We armed ourselves with ropes. She plodded stiffly out of her sty, blinking in the sun, as good as gold, rooting around on the path, following it faithfully – until it went downhill.

We encouraged her with a bucket of tasty slops, and she went for it. But when it moved away down the hill, she stopped. She blinked at us. We wondered what to do.

We would have to use the truck. Paul set off to get it. We hovered around her. She was suspicious; she no longer let us scratch her back.

We waited, glad when the truck was parked above her on the road. We laughed at her as she stood there knock-kneed, jerking her head from left to right, her ears flapping over her small, weak eyes. I felt her embarrassment and fear. We should get it over with, spare her this indignity. I moved forward with a rope.

And she went. Three hundred pounds of her. She brushed Luc and Voyou aside and took off up the mountain. Paul waved his arms helplessly as she came up to the truck but she went straight past him, squealing as he grabbed at her haunches. She went on up.

It was very funny. We all stood and laughed. When the laughter died away, there were three hundred pounds of ham and sausage on the loose and the winter was long.

'Sorry,' I looked up at the sky. Voyou grinned.

'She's yours. Go and get her.'

They got ropes and planks, and I led them up the mountain. I sent scouts out to left and right on the flanks. It was a great joke – the English gentleman-farmer hunting a domestic sow. They loved it.

She was discovered, a hundred feet up. The tracking wasn't exactly difficult. They stood in a wide circle, waiting for my orders, while she snuffled happily and cocked her snout up to the evening air.

'What do you think?' I conferred with Luc.

'I don't know. I've never done this before.' Luc was amused.

'We'll have to get her tied up,' I announced.

'Ah, is that all?' Voyou laughed.

'Ropes!' I shouted to the circle, motioning them all to move in. They did so, and then we rushed her.

It was a noisy fight. The hindquarters were comparatively easy, but her head was strongly defended by teeth and the strength in her neck. She screeched like a siren. After five minutes it was a stalemate. Her hind legs were roped and secure, her front legs tangled in rope and not secure. Henri was lying next to her, grappling with her jaws to keep them shut. Voyou was being thrown from side to side by her neck. She wasn't conquered and she certainly wasn't going to march submissively down from the field of battle. On the other hand, she wasn't going anywhere on two legs.

But no one wanted to spend the night with her.

'*Bordel à que.*' Voyou gave up and Henri rolled away from the teeth. She lay there, panting and snorting in victory. The girls joked. Voyou scowled.

'Bloody women.'

'How are you getting on?' Frédérique hung over his shoulders.

'We're not getting on.' Voyou was angry.

'Shame,' she said playfully.

'Isn't she ugly! What a horror . . . ' Christine giggled.

The male stock was at a low point. Luc moved forward. The sow bucked her head up at him, the torrential shrieking started again. He knelt by her hind legs and patted her. She screamed. He lifted her tail and gently rubbed his finger in and around her cunt. The scream became a squeal, the squeal became a grunt, the grunt became a snuffle and she relaxed into bliss.

'It's disgusting.' Christine turned away.

'You like it, so does she.'

'Even he likes it,' Pierre observed.

We laughed and Luc backed away.

'That calms her down,' Paul was practical, 'but it doesn't solve the transport problem.'

Belline stepped forward for the women.

'You'll just have to carry her.'

'*Merde!*' Voyou snorted. 'Sausage is good, but it's not a religion.'

It was, however, the only answer. We brought up an old door-frame and nailed three thick joists across. We tickled and teased her until she rolled on to it, we roped her down and jerked her on to our shoulders. She travelled back in style, with the occasional protesting bowel movement over her porters. The girls had their gleeful revenge, half the village had assembled joyfully by the truck to watch; and the six men were put firmly in their place, the one of her regal with her new status.

'Don't have any more ideas, please,' Voyou warned me as we queued for the shower. 'Just relax here. This is a peaceful place. A pig is only a pig. Think of beauty or something; or don't think.'

They were sad to understand that I was leaving. It wasn't just at losing me – I felt touched by this – but it stirred hints of discontent in all of them. They didn't like to see it. They thought that I was mad; I thought so too. Why leave? It was stupid. They ignored me, as if I wasn't there. I understood this. It was best that I go as quickly as possible.

'What day is it?'

'Tuesday, Thursday – who cares?' Voyou won another game of backgammon.

'I'll go with Marc and Belline when they do the market.'

'Yes? Where?' Voyou rolled a cigarette.

'I don't know.'

'Home?'

'What?'

'Not a good question, perhaps . . . ' Voyou fiddled with the dice.

'Not at the moment. Another game?' I asked.

'One more.' Voyou let the dice avalanche down the palm of his hand and into a stationary six and one. *'Bon, eh?'*

Friday morning, I washed what clothes I had. They would be dry by early afternoon. I marked myself down to take the goats out to pasture and I left half-way through the lunchtime siesta. I pushed open the stable door and called to them.

'Viens-là, viens-là, mes biques . . . '

They trailed after me, along the dusty road and up above the cows. I left them to eat at their own pace; I settled in the shade with my book, reading quickly from the beginning. It wasn't a bad book, a bit old-fashioned. The kids were tempted to nibble at it if I left it lying by my side while I looked out at the mountains, slumbering in the haze.

The goats climbed slowly upwards. I waited until I could see them no longer; I followed the sound of their bells until I came upon them again. They looked at me, twenty-six heads poked above the tall grass, two or three bleats of recognition.

We meandered; this way and that, through clumps of wild flowers, in amongst the trees and over piles of loose rock. We reached a stream, far on the right of the mountain. They looked warily at the noise and the rushing water. I leapt across and encouraged them. They stood in dismay. I jumped back again; I jumped back-

Jewels

wards and forwards. The goats looked at me in amazement, their ears pricked. I laughed. They suddenly bolted a few yards up the mountain and stood, watching.

This was a nuisance. It was someone else. And when he or she went, I would have a job to stop the goats following them.

It was Françoise. She greeted the goats, moving through them softly, stroking them.

'*Salut, ma bique, salut . . .* '

Their heads dropped and they looked again for food. She came and sat by me.

'Ah, that is what the English do on their own; they jump around like Herbie.' Her eyes twinkled.

'Yes.' I laughed. I had never really talked to her before, our paths hadn't crossed. She was usually severe, and Henri's approach to work had rubbed off on her.

'Reading . . . ?' she smiled.

'Not at the hay . . . ?' I asked her, offering her the tobacco.

'I don't smoke.' She sighed in dismay at the habit.

'Of course not. I'd forgotten.'

'No, I got tired of the hay. I often do, I like to stroll over the mountain. I usually take the goats out. No one else seems to want to do it, so that's fine.'

She pulled her hat down on her head. She didn't take the sun as easily as she took her lovers, her face was red.

'So you are going tomorrow.'

'Yes.'

'What I came to say, on my travels, is that if you would like to make love tonight before you go, I would like to . . . ' She paused and gave me a friendly, warm look. 'And if not, perhaps we can make love sometimes when you come back.'

'*Oui, je le veux bien,*' I said, looking under that hat for her.

'That will be good.' She took my wrist and caressed it

123

lightly. 'We will have a fire tonight on the mountain, and we will go to bed early because there is always tomorrow. There will be a bag of sausage and cheese downstairs by the cooker for you. We thought that you should take four hundred francs. Unless you need more?' she asked.

Money. I hadn't thought about money for a long time, I hadn't thought about it at all. The little you could get for money; the number of needs that had disappeared in this place. I knew that they had accounts and reckonings. No one bothered. It was a kind of game.

'No,' I said, 'I'm all right for money.'

Françoise nodded. 'Don't drink a lot tonight.' She waved a finger at me as she stood up.

'No, I won't.'

'And don't get lost on the mountain,' she called over her shoulder.

'Don't lose the hay,' I shouted.

'We won't.'

I watched her disappear. She turned and shooed the goats away from her. They ran, frightened, up towards me. She waved and was lost to sight.

Page 110. And a half. I left the book on a rock and followed the animals. The sun was falling now. Strange how it took the life out of the air with it. It would soon be time to go down.

I led the goats in a wide sweep across the mountain, up above the terraces where I could see Belline, Françoise, Pierre and Annie roping up the last of the bales. I had never spoken much to Belline. I regretted. It was rude. I laughed at myself.

And to my right, Marc transferring the bales from cable to cable, waving far down at Paul while Voyou and Luc staggered towards the barn. I could just see their legs underneath the mass of hay. Further down, Christine, a solitary figure, watering the garden; Henri coming up the path towards her with a bundle of firewood. He hadn't noticed her yet. She might just be scowling, now.

Sure enough, she looked across at the passing figure. I smiled. The goats were waiting. They were bored. '*Viens-là, viens . . .*' It was time to go down and get washed.

They were thirteen at milking, and thirteen on the mountain, laughing, drinking and eating around the fire. It was a warm night; with no cloud and a small moon over the jawbone. Pierre played the guitar and they sang. We were joined again by the two young shepherds, and those who wished to get drunk did so fairly rapidly. Those who didn't drifted off from the fire, bending to shake hands with me, the girls with their kisses. Good luck, I whispered. Luck?! They laughed. Thank you, Frédérique said.

'Pierre is sleeping in your room,' Françoise squeezed my shoulder.

'Ten minutes,' I said.

There were six of us left at the fire. Voyou tinkered with the guitar; the shepherds closed in on Christine. She sat with her legs bunched up. They talked of her beautiful eyes, Christine, Christine; she wore that ugly trapped look. Luc sang to Voyou. Her forehead was folded with worry, the shadows flickered across it over the fire. All the world desired her, she had an attraction. She looked up at one of the shepherds and used it for an instant; something he said, she giggled coyly and hid her face in her knees.

I lay back down on the stubble, looking at the nothing in the sky. I was drowsy with the wine, but not drunk. It was comfortable. I was in good shape, back amongst myself. There was laughter.

I said goodbye quickly to Christine, bending to kiss her on both cheeks. She was surprised that I was going; it was the first she had heard of it, she pretended. She scolded me. She insisted on the third, lovers', kiss. The shepherds guffawed.

'Come to England in the winter,' I smiled.

'*Oh là là*,' she laughed.

'*Au revoir*.'

'*Bon voyage, mon petit Anglais*.'

I shook hands with the shepherds. They tried to detain me with the bottle, but no. Then Luc; a couple of slaps and a nodding of heads. Voyou laughed. 'He's drunk. He won't be scything tomorrow.'

'Four o'clock,' Luc protested, 'four o'clock, we'll see who's there.'

Voyou roared with laughter. He stood up to shake hands with me, most formal and polite.

'*La bonne route, eh?*'

'*Toi aussi*.'

'*Bof! Pas moi! Je suis tranquil ici. Tu reviendras*.'

'*Oui*,' I smiled at the scruffy, toothless figure.

'*Je te le dis. Tu reviendras. C'est sûr. C'est obligé*; it is obliged, my friend. And then you will see the little Voyou, also without any teeth. You will come back. *Vas-y; la bonne route*. We will drink to you at Christmas. In fact, as soon as you go, we can start drinking to you. *Vas-y!* Tac-a-tac tac.'

I hugged him and stumbled away down the mountain. I waited ten minutes in front of the washing mirror. I was English, stiff upper lip, entirely composed. I went upstairs to the warmth of Françoise's bed, where she gave me the beauty of the tenderly opening crocus; and we slept.

It was dark. I heard the clump of the scythers' boots as they moved down the corridor and out of the door. I heard them in the kitchen and I heard them leave, the clang of the blades as they came out of the rack, the low whistles to the dogs; and it was quiet again. Françoise was turned towards me, her arm across my side, sleeping peacefully with the warm, humid scent of love.

It was grey light. Marc was shaking me. 'We leave in

fifteen minutes.' I was shaken again. I confirmed. Marc left the room. I pulled myself awake. I slipped out from under the arm. She tugged sleepily.
'*La bonne route*,' she whispered. 'Come back.'
'*Bien sûr.*'
She fell away into her sleep.
I had two plastic bags. I scribbled '*Merci*' on the blackboard; then rubbed it out, imagining Voyou's face. We weaved down the mountainside in the car, the headlights two glimmers of yellow which bobbed in front of us. We stopped at the bottom of the valley, on the main road. A truck roared past on its way to Italy. The car shook.
'*Vas-y. À la prochaine.*'
'*À la prochaine.*'
'*'Revoir.*'
It wasn't the place to meet Belline. I scrambled out of the car. They drove off. A short blast on the horn. I waved. They were hidden by another truck, coming towards me. I put up my thumb. It flashed its headlights and the sound of the engine didn't drop. It went past, pulling the hair off my face with the draught and scattering pebbles against my shins.
I stepped back, out of the vacuum, shocked. The truck faded away, its red lights indifferent to the sunrise. The road was silent and empty. I put my hand in the polythene bag and squeezed the package of cheese for comfort. I rolled a cigarette unsteadily. When I reached the Swiss frontier that night, I searched for my passport. In a panic, through the polythene. The customs man helped. It was he who finally held it up, smiling. I was looking at the four hundred francs, bitterly grateful.

Tourist Attraction

FROM THE Belvedere Fortress at the end of the day, the noise seemed to become heavy with evening and fall back to the earth. The city resumed her quiet self-possession. It was as if she had spent the day on her knees, looking into a teeming mirror, and was relieved now to straighten up in the shade of the cypress hills with her poise rediscovered. She had been oppressed by the bundles of dazed admirers which were thrown down in front of her, and tormented by the bustle of her servants who supposedly sustained her by selling her image. It was a deliverance to be able to get up off her knees, to stop being gaped at and scrutinised and probed and bought. At this evening moment she had her dignity; she rested, indifferent to her customers.

Said had long since stopped being sensitive to what Florence might or might not feel towards her servants. He was glad to get into a car on Sundays and leave the whole dirty bedlam behind him. He crossed in front of the *duomo* to get from one side of the city to the other, and his only interest in the Belvedere was the conviction that his boss wouldn't relegate him to the small market stall at the toenails of the greater David.

For Said was the best salesman that Giulio had ever employed; he sold more onyx eggs, more plaster Davids and more plastic ashtrays than anyone else in the San Lorenzo market. Giulio was under the impression that he was the only person who knew this, but Said knew exactly what moved where in the Florence markets and he therefore knew that he was irreplaceable.

It perturbed Giulio that Said negotiated his percentage

with more insight into the profits than himself, and that was after Giulio had wasted his weekend poring over the books to the wailings of his five children from the garden of their house in the hills.

He spent Saturday evening going through the bundles of money that he took off Said. The money was good. Giulio had to admit it. There was always more than one could expect from the Lord. But he wasn't happy, he was suspicious. He was certain that he was being swindled. He knew that he was not very sharp, and if you weren't very sharp then you were being swindled; it was a rule of life.

The fact of the matter was that Said sold the rubbish off Giulio's stall at a price some 20 per cent higher than any of the other stalls. Giulio couldn't believe it. Even as he watched Said, that Friday, even as he stood to one side, uncertain, while Said wished a young German couple a happy honeymoon after having sold them two statues for three thousand lire more than the stall fifty yards away was asking, Giulio still thought it must be a stroke of luck, the couple must be uniquely stupid, it couldn't happen again; he crossed himself. Said must be swindling him with this high wage he kept twisting out of him, it wasn't right, he would have to take the matter in hand, they would get on a regular *padrone*-worker basis, like the other stalls. There was something wrong somewhere.

And so, early Monday morning, there was a short scene in the San Lorenzo market which could be lost amongst the bustle of traders setting up their stalls. But it was always there, it was a ritual, though neither Said nor Giulio recognised it as such or thought to invoke the result of the previous Monday's dispute.

Said was up at six and had dragged the stall barrow out of the lock-up garage by seven-thirty. He was having to sell the left-overs from last week and was cursing Giulio for his inefficiency.

Meanwhile, fortified by a last-minute harangue from his ample wife, Giulio tried to steer the new Fiat pick-up through the market, outraged by his inability to control the clutch, terrified by the size of the monster and convinced that the old simple days, before Arab salesmen, were so much easier.

'Where have you been?' Said was at the back doors of the van before Giulio had switched off the engine, and was carrying the boxes to their innocuous position just inside the doorway of a block of flats. It wouldn't do to have fifty of the same rare statues on display at the same time.

'You pampered brat . . .' Giulio hissed at him as they crossed. He waited in the cool shade of the portico, gibbering venomously.

Said didn't reappear. Giulio ventured out into the sunlight and noise. Said was selling. The van was blocking the narrow street. Giulio pushed himself in front of a tourist with a rough '*Scusi*,' and the tourist was frightened off.

'Hey, just one minute, I do you a good deal, just for you . . .' Said called. The tourist waved her hand in dismissal. Said glared back at Giulio.

'Unload the van; we'll get that done, then I want to talk with you.' Giulio felt firm.

'*You* unload your mother-of-God van, it's not my job,' Said blazed with anger. 'You know what you do? You put off the customers. I lose a lot of money.' His jabbing finger stopped just short of Giulio's chest.

'Whose money?' Giulio spluttered. '*My* money. You take, take; you leave me nothing, no profit, nothing . . .'

'Eh . . .' Said spread his arms out wide and looked at the heavens.

'We sell what *I* buy.' Giulio asserted Said's dependence, and rubbed his hands victoriously. The cars bleated for him to move the van off the road.

130

'*I* sell.' Said's eyes narrowed.

Three feet away from each other, each one with a hand on the van, they shouted and screamed and called upon the heavens to witness injustice and ingratitude. The tourists were amused; the workers had seen it all before. A traffic policeman appeared in a splendid strutting cameo. Giulio stamped round to the driver's seat. Said followed him.

'You couldn't even keep chickens.'

'You're fired.' Giulio slammed the door.

'Good.'

There was then an interlude, while Giulio jumped the van round the block with his hand on the horn, scattering pedestrians and dogs. And Said spat into the road and started working on the convenient gathering of spectators, harrying them to buy a freshly delivered icon, as if they owed it to him for the entertainment. Between the rounds there were always a couple of good sales to greet the irate, unshaven *padrone* who jerked to a halt in the same place some ten minutes later. He ignored Said. He panted out with the boxes, crucifying himself ostentatiously. Said went over to him.

'And what in God's name do you think you're doing?' Giulio squeezed out over the top of a dozen Greek heroes.

'I don't want to see you with a heart attack, you old miser; and you're blocking the street again.'

'You want your job back, eh?'

'I don't care. I can make more money in the other market.'

'Careful with that box. You think I'm made of money?'

'Yes.'

'We talk about it in the bar.'

And that was the end of the normal Monday street ritual. Said and Giulio arrived at exactly the same terms as before over a coffee in the bar behind the stall; Said exasperated at the waste of selling-time, Giulio begrudging every inevitable per cent. Then Said would step out into the oven of the San Lorenzo market, while Giulio stayed inside the bar, groaning to his fellow proprietors about the working day and the responsibilities. He'd occasionally hover at the corner of the stall, smiling. He might even open his mouth to a young girl. Until Said scowled at him. He'd pat Said on the back at noon and drive up to the hills for a siesta; such was the weight of responsibility. He'd return for the takings when Said packed up at seven in the evening.

On the way home, Giulio might stop off at the stall on the Belvedere Fortress, where there was less holocaust and a bit of a cooling breeze for his son; and sometimes then it occurred to him that Florence was beautiful. It was home; his family had lived there for generations. How peaceful it must have been as peasants, throwing grain out for the chickens. But you'd never get a van and a car and a larger house from scattering grain; and you could never keep women happy whatever you did.

Once a month, their irritation swirled so fiercely that they did fly apart, each swearing the most sacred oaths never to work together again, each denouncing the other – convinced of treachery and deceit. Said's pride was bitterly insulted by Giulio's careless assumption that he was dishonest; Giulio took Said's refusal to join him for a drink as a blatant rejection of the truce flag. The argument spluttered across the increasing distance between them.

In the middle of July, Said decided to throw a statue at Giulio, to the delight of everybody; and then paid for it, to a similarly widespread astonishment – not least because he handed over about a fifth of the usual selling price.

Giulio pocketed the money before noticing the lull

around him as people calculated their respect. He stamped round to the other side of the stall and sat on a stool, chattering to himself and to anyone who happened to pause in front of him. Said stood in the middle of the street, one hand on his chin, the other on his hip; he watched Giulio selling nothing and Giulio's apparent indifference. Giulio was careful to avoid Said's eyes. There was a stalemate.

And then, at the end of the street, there appeared a rare gaggle of Japanese. Now, if you sold a statue to one Japanese, it was quite possible that the entire party would do their shopping at your stall; they might even all buy the same statue. They were peculiar like that.

They were forty. They swayed through the market place like a blob of mercury. The tension of expectation rippled closer; eyes twitched discreetly, *padroni* peeled themselves out of the shade, Americans came to be ignored. They must have arrived from London, because there were twenty-five shoulder bags which had 'I am a kinky nippon tourist' printed in large white letters on the side.

Said couldn't *not* sell; it wasn't in his nature. He minced over to the stall where I worked. We ended up offloading thirty-five strings of raffia fruit and a dozen gruesome leather wallets while Giulio hopped up and down in anger. It cost Giulio considerable self-abasement to get Said back over to his side of the street.

Raffia fruit wasn't likely to engage Said's attention, there wasn't enough money in it. So I was surprised when he started to take a whimsical half-hour away from Giulio's stall to sell our down-market collection of souvenirs. He enjoyed talking and he obviously enjoyed instructing me on the skills of selling. He seemed to be pleased to find someone else on the market who wasn't Italian. He regarded the Italians with a deep suspicion and sometimes with scorn. He couldn't understand why

Giulio tried to chisel away at his terms of employment. This, he felt, was merely dishonourable, and typically Italian. He wanted to talk to another foreigner about it. And then he wanted to learn as much English as possible, because he was going to Los Angeles to sell cars. He was going to get married to an American girl in the autumn and get a work permit and sell cars. In Los Angeles. Americans were rich and would buy anything from him; an American couldn't walk past him without buying.

' . . . especially the women.' Said was so sure of himself that he didn't even wink. We had been friends for a week. I laughed.

'You want to see? You don't believe me? I show you, Robert. You watch. Then you learn.'

A browsing threesome was approaching from the left; the quieter sort of Americans; middle-income Cook's bracket; husband, wife and daughter. Said engrossed the father and daughter in leather-worked bottles, and while I took the money he already had the mother away on the other side of the street and had sold her a statue before her husband had his wallet back in his pocket.

Said shrugged as they walked away satisfied. 'You don't think I could get rich in America?'

'I've met salesmen in Los Angeles,' I warned him; 'they're good. And you won't be selling to tourists.'

'No difference. Americans buy anything from me.' He stalked off.

'And you haven't got a work permit.'

Said walked across to check on a child who was gaping at the onyx eggs. He gave her one. The child ran to its mother. The mother was angry. Said graciously refused to accept a thousand lire for the egg. Once. He managed to overcome his generosity at the second time of asking. He came back, motioning me into a doorway behind the stall. I checked with Giorgio, my *padrone*, who waved me away for a break.

'Let's get an ice-cream,' I offered.

'Robert...' Said tapped me on the shoulder and looked round to see that no one was listening. 'I am in love.' He shook his head seriously.

'Congratulations,' I said. 'She isn't American, is she?'

'How you guess?' Said grinned.

'Rich?' I suggested.

His eyes steeled and he crossed his arms.

'You are typical European. Corrupt. How do I know if she is rich? I don't ask her. I don't take any money from her. I pay for her – apartment, car, food . . . everything. She is in love with me. She is more in love with me than I am; I tell you, Robert.'

'Said, no one could be more in love with you than you are.'

'I do not understand.' We reached the door of the bar down the street; very few of the workers drank in the same bar as the *padroni*.

'It doesn't matter; it's a joke.'

'No. What does it mean? I must speak English very well before we go to America. What does it mean? That I am in love with myself? That is stupid. It is only possible for the Italians . . . *limone*.' He leaned against the bar. 'You want one?'

'Yes, I'll get them.'

'No. I pay. *Due spremute di limone.*'

'Don't you ever let anyone pay for anything?' It was a habit of his.

'Lousy salesmen do not make good money. You teach me English.'

'O.K.'

'Sure, man.' Said translated it into American.

We waited for the pressed lemons and then took them to the back of the bar. Said immediately checked his watch.

'Well, where is she?' I asked him. 'I've never seen her.'

135

He grabbed my arm and squeezed it.

'You think I bring her here? To the market?' he demanded.

'Why not?' I attempted to disengage my wrist.

'Because it is corrupt here. And I know when it is corrupt. Believe me. You see this . . . and this' – the scars on his arm and face – ' . . . knife. Many, many fights; and in prison; four, maybe five against me.' He glanced suspiciously round the room as though we were in some bad spy film. I couldn't think of anything to say. It was he who got the most exorbitant prices on the market. He took my silence as agreement.

'You understand? That is good. Some day maybe I will introduce you to her. Have you finished? Then we go.'

I didn't have time to finish the drink; we walked quickly back to the market place, Said calling out to the ladies when he was still ten yards away from the stall. 'Stupid people . . . ' was the last thing he muttered under his breath as I passed him.

Well, it explained why he never stopped after clearing away the stall and why he played his Sundays very close to his chest. I wondered if he thought she would be embarrassed or offended by his system of flirting with the customers. She needn't have worried. Almost everyone else who worked in the market spent the summer going haywire with self-indulgence; the commodities were plentiful. But Said was faithful, annually so, according to Giulio. And always going to America; Giulio shrugged. No papers. Said had been in Florence for three years. Giulio smiled. Said hadn't even got any papers for Italy. Giulio shrugged again.

There was a fortnight during which we didn't seem to have much contact. I was aware of being watched. Said visited Giorgio's stall once or twice; you couldn't say he was cold, but it was as if he were considering me for a job.

Then the invitation occurred. I had passed some secret test.

'You come to eat? Saturday, after we finish. I show you where I live. You bring a girl, a nice girl.' Said cautioned with one finger.

'All right,' I grinned.

I found one half-way through Friday; a dark-haired American girl, about nineteen or twenty. She was attractive. I sold her a bargain. She was suspicious but she was interested. We arranged ourselves for Saturday. She didn't buy anything from Said. He came over immediately.

'That is a nice girl; one hell of a nice girl.' We watched her drift away down the street.

'Yeah, she's coming to eat tomorrow. O.K.?' I laughed.

'You know, Robert, I have ask her too.'

'Why?'

'I wasn't thinking you know any nice girls.'

'What did she say?'

'She tells me she already has a date. You should marry her. She likes you. She would be good for you.'

'Thank you,' I said. 'She's staying at the Hilton; she's not very likely to marry me.'

'My friend . . . ', Said laid a hand on my shoulder, 'don't give up hope. Always have hope.'

'You've got a customer,' I pointed him back to his stall.

It was never any trouble working for Giorgio and the percentages were sorted out into hard cash as soon as he decided that he'd had enough of the market on Saturday evening. I didn't cost him very much. I got the stall packed away and helped him pull it into our lock-up. We wished each other a peaceful Sunday, and that was the end of the week's work.

Said was exasperated with Giulio. They had completely different concepts of mathematics.

'Hey, listen, I'll see you in a couple of hours,' I parted them.

'Sure, man.'

'*Ciao*, Robert . . . ' Giulio beamed in the attempt to establish an alliance. Said stepped between us.

'Now you mean bastard . . . '

Giulio blinked at the English, and I left them to get on with the war.

It was a beautiful walk home on a Saturday evening; the piazzas were littered with trash, but there weren't many tourists about. You could feel that you belonged to the place for a moment or two, away from the market hustle and the pressure of the heat. I took a meandering zig-zag across town in front of the *duomo*, through the flower market to the river, then over the Ponte Vecchio and up the hill to the Piazza Pitti near which I shared a flat with a researching Scotsman. It worked very well because we were rarely there at the same time, except to sleep. It was too much of a good thing to sit on a set of steps somewhere and watch the ebb and flow of the world, or try and figure out what on earth was happening on Italian television from behind a pinball machine in the bar downstairs. Occasionally the Scotsman and I would get devastatingly drunk somewhere and mumble about Existence.

He was always stunningly correct with anyone he found in our kitchen in the morning; he had a beard and a long dressing-gown. He also had a tendency to argue with policemen, and he was so broke that I had to fish him out of jail twice over the summer. It seemed like a fair return for his allowing girls into a space which he held to be the sanctuary for his renaissance.

I had a glass of red in the bar downstairs and then fell asleep to the sound of his thesis tap-dancing through the wall. He didn't bother to wake me, he just showed her in, switched on the light, and retreated to think.

'Robert . . . '

'Laurie?'

'Hi. Did you remember?'

Yes. She was tall, beautiful thick black hair over her shoulders and she wasn't the type of girl who got lost in a room. She was bloody angry. She wasn't the slightest bit interested in looking round the flat, or in taking a chair to alleviate her impact.

'Of course I remembered. I had a long day. Sorry. What time is it?'

'About half after eight.'

'That's not the end of the world.'

'It is, with the Italians in that bar downstairs.'

'I'm sorry. I'll have a wash and we'll go.'

'Do you want to?'

'Of course I do.'

The evening had started badly and I suddenly couldn't think of anything more wasteful than sitting with Said.

'I bought some wine,' Laurie said. 'I'm not sure if it's any good.'

I had my head under the kitchen tap. The Scotsman opened his door.

'Will that be three for dinner?' he asked with incisive politeness.

'No. We're going out.'

'I see.' His door closed. I went back to the bedroom. Laurie stood with the Chianti bottle.

'That's good wine. I don't know if Said ever drinks.'

'Well he can be a friend, can't he?'

'I hope so.'

'What are you looking at?'

'You. What did you do today?' I searched for a cleaner shirt, exasperated with the evening. I didn't feel like meeting anyone else.

'I sat around the hotel, then there was a visit to the museum.'

'The unfinished Michelangelos?'

'I guess so.'

I laughed. She sat on the bed.

'The statues were beautiful. And the carpets were beautiful. But the statues were so *serious*. Two whole lines of serious statues. Don't you people know how to enjoy yourselves?'

My shirt was lop-sided because the buttons were all one buttonhole higher than they should have been. I never wake up in the mood to appreciate challenges.

'And what do you do? London, Brussels, Paris, Madrid, Rome, Florence; one after another?' It was my choleric hangover tone. I don't know why she didn't walk out. She paused for a minute. I thought she was on her way. But she spoke.

'And Prague and a boat-ride down the Rhine – that was good – and we went to Oxford.'

'Oh? How was Oxford?' was all I could think to say, looking at her.

'It was really good,' she nodded.

'That's good.' I smiled. This was going to be one of those intellect-stretching evenings.

'Are we going?' she asked.

'Yeah, let's go. We'll walk down to the river and get a taxi.'

When we got outside, I put an arm round her loosely and we were both relieved at the contact, slumping against each other and relaxing for the stroll down the hill.

'Let's make a rule not to say anything.' She smiled largely and looked straight ahead.

'Well, not for half an hour. It might be difficult after that. It would be a bit strange to arrive at Said's in dead silence as though we were about to get a divorce.'

She laughed.

She wanted to pay for the taxi, and the driver had his eye on charging her double. It wouldn't have made much impact on that valueless roll of notes; she thought that he looked poor and anyway the cab was cheaper than in the States. Laurie didn't care less and she didn't want protecting. I knew Florence too well.

'O.K., O.K.; you'll get taken for a ride.'

'If I want to get taken for a ride, you let me. This is the first time I've gotten away from the hotel and I'm enjoying it. So there! Let's have fun.' And a smile spread over the taxi-driver's face. He even managed to know exactly where Said lived and banged on the door of the flat for us before rushing back down the stairs.

Said threw open the door and there was a burst of fraternal hugging in place of introductions.

'Nice girl, beautiful girl . . . ' Said held Laurie at arm's length. In fact, he was amazed that she was as tall as him, and disconcerted that we were both in jeans and a shirt. He always found it difficult to understand why Anglo-Saxons dressed so sloppily when they were so rich.

It was a small, self-contained flat that had been modernised out of the old Via dei Servi buildings and furnished haphazardly from the more expensive chain-stores. It was tidy and quiet and obvious that the television had just been switched off and the ashtrays emptied. Said led us into the living-room and showed us both to a seat. Laurie refused a cigarette. I lit one. He was alive with energy, even after a full day in the market. He dashed out to get glasses, then forgot them and sat talking to Laurie. His eyes charmed her. He broke off mid-way through a sentence.

'Carol is my girlfriend; she is just come home now. Very busy, you know. I call her. Carol! Robert is here with Laurie.'

The bedroom door opened almost immediately; she must have been waiting for him to cue her. It was so extraordinary that I stood up without thinking, wondering what to do with the cigarette. Laurie tucked her legs up under her. Said was confused. It was completely out of line with his culture to stand up when a woman came into the room, and yet there was so much energy in him for sympathy and he was so anxious to put everyone at their ease, that he sprang out of the chair and led Carol in, as if she were an invalid. She shook herself free of all the attention.

'Oh honey, you didn't get the glasses for the wine.'

'I don't remember the glasses in the kitchen . . . ' Said dropped her angrily and went out, flicking his cigarette and shaking his head.

'He's a little hyped-up tonight; we don't have people round here that often.' Carol looked at Laurie cautiously; there were at least ten years between them and they chose very different styles. Laurie was featured enough not to bother with cosmetics or clothes or manners, and Carol was very aware that on her own she was plain.

They bantered. Carol was generous with herself. She made it clear that it was her apartment and that Said was her man. She had an acute way of establishing these precepts inside the apparently low-level conversation. It didn't look as though the two girls would get along very well. But Said's enthusiasm was boundless and this carried the evening. It was presumably his choice of food and his cooking because the meal was preceded by a detailed explanation of the Arab menu. He only picked while the rest of us ate ravenously, much to his delight.

The conversation was mostly between him and Laurie, with a persistence that indicated their complete lack of interest in each other. They talked about America, and Carol stayed out of the arena, chain-smoking and playing with her hair. She seemed to want to make it clear that Said embarrassed her. I felt sorry for him, but it fitted an endless future of Teach-Yourself-English records and T.V. dinners in the Los Angeles suburbs.

We finished eating and it was time to get rid of the formality. Said decided to throw the dishes out of the

142

window. They went down three flights and disintegrated in the back courtyard. Laurie laughed and Carol smiled as Said posed heroically in front of her.

'Honey . . . '

Said grinned with pride. 'Tonight we are engaged to be married.' Carol smiled at Laurie. 'Then we go to America, we make a lot of money and have children, three four.' Carol took his hand.

'Boys,' she pronounced.

'Not important in America. Boys, girls, anything you like.'

It was a bizarre announcement. Their spirit was festive but not entirely confident. We kissed Carol and drank to their happiness. Laurie wanted to share.

'Come, Robert, I show you something.' Said went into the bedroom. It was a good opportunity for the girls to talk. Carol seemed to feel miles from home and rather frightened. Laurie was well on top of the wine and the lack of hotel frigidity. I followed Said with a glass.

'I like Carol,' I said.

'She is tired. We are very happy. She has come back from Padova.' Said pulled open a drawer.

'Padua? What happens in Padua?' I wondered.

'Padova, Verona, Venezia . . . very beautiful. She take the car, she likes to go for one week, maybe two. I give her money. She will give me money in America until I find a job.'

'Are you sure?' He looked sure but he looked sad.

'Please, Robert,' he turned, 'I want to get out of this fuck country. She loves me. I love her. We get married and we get papers. We both go together. That is love. You think she is beautiful?'

'Yes.'

'She is beautiful. I am happy. You want to see knives for fighting? Look here at these knives.'

Six of them were laid on black velvet inside the drawer;

from the simple stiletto to an elaborately carved scimitar that would have seemed camp to a ritual assassin. I was a bit drunk. I touched a blade lightly, leaving a fingerprint. They were hostile objects.

'Sharp?'

'You bet.' Said picked up the stiletto and slipped through a pinch of my hair. 'Very sharp. You can bet.'

'Do you use them?' I asked him.

'No more. Now they sleep. Very pretty, but no more. Too many scars.' He smiled peacefully, as a man in retirement contemplates a newspaper. 'Very much trouble with Fascists. My father and brother all dead. Four brother killed by the Government. My father in prison.' He patted me on the back, smiling again at my being distracted into sympathy. 'The King is very cruel, my friend, very cruel. We fight. But it was stupid with a knife.' He laughed. 'Now I will go to America and get money and then I will kill them. That is for us, you and I. The woman is not to tell, Robert. The woman has no feeling for this, she has no memory.' He closed the drawer and locked it.

'What happened to your passport?'

'No passport. There was a big fight. I kill two men. Then I get a boat. No papers. I work for the son of a bitch Giulio. Three years. Then I am in love. So. The papers will come when we are married. Then fuck to Italy. You think it is sad? No. It is sad for my mother. My father was a strong man, very strong man. But stupid. Not modern. It is better to sell cars to the rich Americans. She is rich, your American?'

'I expect so.' I nodded.

'That is good. Mine no. But beautiful and I will make money. More beautiful than your woman. You think so?'

'No.'

'That is good. Your woman is too young. But rich. Maybe you will marry.' He considered.

144

'Tomorrow,' I assured him.

'After tonight.' He grinned.

'Nice flat, Said, you've got a nice place.' We moved towards the door.

'Nice apartment, nice car, nice woman, wrong country; you think so too?' he encouraged Carol.

She patted the carpet next to her and Said settled down for a moment. Then he was up and off to make tea. I sat. I stroked Laurie's back. It was uncomplicated. They talked about Europe and the places they had visited. There was a sort of pecking order amongst tourists and Carol was fairly well-placed due to Said's car, which enabled her to get out into the countryside and as far as France and Germany. In any case, she had been in Europe for three months. And she was determined to enjoy it, as any deprived person would. She was thirsty. She had saved and it was the chance of a lifetime to get an education.

She obviously wanted to talk and Said was pleased that there was someone who could talk to her in good English. He poked round the room like a highly strung greyhound, but you could see that he was satisfied with himself that he had made the correct choice of guests.

Carol pushed Laurie into talking. She wasn't as shallow as she seemed. It was just her resentment. She was quite able to pinpoint paintings from the Uffizi and the Louvre although, being younger and the victim of force-feeding, it suited her to be blasé until she found someone who was enthusiastic. Art had been very definitely put in the opposite corner to life. You couldn't blame her. The tour of Europe was like a *post mortem* operation. She could have had it all out of the coroner's report. It demanded docility and her lack of this was endearing. After five weeks, she'd had enough; her instinct for self-preservation was too strong. Carol was sympathetic, though slightly amused by the afflictions of the rich. It was a world she had been envious of, back in the States. And now she was close to Said, and grateful for his support. Various feelings of unease and security floated to and fro.

It was a successful evening, ages and nationalities melting together. We decided to take the car and go up into the hills with a picnic, spend the Sunday out of town. Said was delighted.

Laurie and I wouldn't let him drive us home. We ambled back through the town, arms round each other. I was dreamy; she was quiet and frowning. We stopped in the Piazza della Signoria and watched the huge heroes tangling with each other. There were ghosts abroad. Your eyes couldn't move fast enough to catch them shifting in the gloom. We walked over to the Loggia; these dozen vast figures always posing or wrestling in their gallery above the square. As we stopped to look up at them, they froze; each one blank-eyed, muscles straining to hold the stone. It was eerie, the amount of life that was held motionless.

'He's handsome.' Laurie walked over to Perseus, climbed up and slapped him on the thigh. She challenged him and mocked him, tapping her fingernails against his leg as she leant against him.

'Don't embarrass him,' I suggested. 'He can't do anything about it; he's powerless.'

'He wouldn't do anything about it even if he wasn't made of metal; would you?' she asked him. 'He's a faggot. Am I allowed to do this?'

'Why?'

'There're two cops on the other side of the square.'

'They'll enjoy the show.'

'Well, I'm not giving them a show, not for free I'm not.'

She did though. She balanced herself on the edge of the plinth and asked me to catch her. She slid down to the ground and waited to be kissed. The *carabinieri* laughed from across the square. One of them clapped his hands. '*Bella . . . bella . . .*'

146

She waved to them and we walked on, down to the river.

'Do you want to go with Said tomorrow?' she asked.

'Yes, I'll go. I want to get out of the city. Anyway I like them both.'

'Yeah.' Laurie sounded rejected.

'What else are you going to do? Don't you want to go?'

She didn't answer. We went several yards and she pushed her arm through mine.

'She's got herself in a bad situation.'

'Oh? Why?'

There was even a moon over the river, and the noise of our footsteps echoed in and out of the gallery. It was the average beautiful night for being alone or in love. I liked Said and Carol just as we had left them at the door, happy to be with each other and not thinking about Government approval.

'She's got herself all tied up with the country and him.'

'Good for her. She wants to give something and she gets a lot out of it.'

'Sure.' Laurie was hurt. We turned left and hurried half way across the Ponte Vecchio, then I stopped.

'What's wrong?' she asked.

'I don't know why you dismiss it, just because you're safely inside an organised six weeks. She can do what she wants to do. Maybe they'll get married, have four children and sell a thousand cars a week. They seem happy together. Both of them could do a lot worse. Give them a chance or leave them alone.' I couldn't think why I adopted the cause; I didn't want to get married and have four children.

'Hell will they get married! No way. She wants out. She came over here to have an affair and it's gotten too heavy. She's all screwed up. And if he doesn't get the papers then she has to worry about getting stuck in Europe.' Laurie knew what she was talking about.

'She does well enough out of it. Some people might just consider that there are better places to live than fucking Los Angeles, or America.' I did, for one, and furiously.

'Yeah . . . it's the vacation; everyone hangs out when they're on vacation . . . ' Laurie tried to calm it down.

'Like you . . . ' I gave her.

She paused. 'I wish I could be living the way she does, even with the hassle when she wants to split. Maybe when I'm through with my art course at college. She'll go back without him.'

'She feels more deeply about him than that. She's thirty-one, thirty-two; she doesn't take vacations.'

'You mean you hope she doesn't.'

I sat on a step and yawned. Laurie slouched over to the parapet and looked out across the river. She had everything tied up now. She had got away from the tour and seen how good the tour was, the value of being confined. I hated tourists. Almost as much as I was sick of Florence.

'Do you have a cigarette, Robert? I don't have any.'

'I didn't know you smoked.'

'I only smoke a cigarette when I'm feeling down . . . '

. . . and gazing over the water, being lost and attractive; hesitant piano, camera zooms in, flare from match lighting up lovely, vulnerable eyes.

'I'm acting,' she said, and coughed. 'I don't like cigarettes. And I'm not down. I guess I'm jealous.' Lovely, vulnerable, questioning eyes. It's a bit tiresome the way women throw over a parcel of provocation and leave you to fumble with the thought that it might explode. Even honesty. It seems to amuse them. It was probably still because I didn't meet her in the bar.

'Why aren't we walking?' She affected a light-heartedness.

'Because the Hilton is back over the bridge along to the left and my bed is straight up the hill.'

148

'Oh. Will you call for me tomorrow?' She was getting worried. 'I'm sorry,' she said fiercely.

'Yes, it's a pity.' I agreed. It was very serious. If she had been older, I would have laughed.

'I get angry, I get so angry, man, I want to shout; it's all so' – she shook her hair wildly – 'slow . . . old games . . . I don't understand. I get so angry I don't know what to do, I hate it so much. Shit, I wish I was back home.'

'Let's go and make love then and stop pissing about with other people's problems in a fourteenth-century street.'

I watched her as she was getting dressed in the half-dawn, when she scrambled out of the warmth of the bed and stretched. She watched herself too, in a contented way. She sat down to put on her sandals, she smiled and then she was serious.

'I guess all the museums just make me feel horny.'

Said had his hand on the horn for nearly a minute before I could get to the window and yell down at him, and I had five minutes to sort out clothes and fall into the back of the car. Said grinned from ear to ear; Carol tapped her ash out of the window.

'You can start driving. She's at the Hilton,' I said flatly.

'No good?' Said turned round in the driver's seat and patted my knee sadly.

'Honey . . . ' Carol was restless. 'Let's go and pick her up.'

'No good is bad.' Said reflected. 'Bad. You want we should look for another girl, Robert?'

'She had to go back to have breakfast with her parents, Said. We're definitely in love, don't worry.'

'That is good. Very good.'

Said let in the clutch and the car took off exuberantly. I was glad that I wasn't sitting in the front seat and that most of Florence was at morning mass. Said had this

149

fixation on second gear between the speeds of zero and fifty, and we howled along the river-bank, courting our own after-life. I tried looking stoically out of the side window, but I wanted to see what we were going to hit. It was better than a pot of coffee for waking you up and frying the nerve ends in the stomach.

'This is a very good car.' Said tapped the steering-wheel amid a fall-out of silence in front of the Hilton. I was having some insight into the meaning of life. Carol was lighting another cigarette from the first one. There were church bells somewhere over the other side of Florence.

'We go in.' Said was in favour.

'I'll go in. How do I look?' There might be parents, and the last ten minutes had ravaged me with transition of one sort and another.

I got out of the car and it was good to be back on dry land. They were waiting in the lobby of the hotel, Laurie simmering with a rosy vitality, the father a friendly bear of a man and the mother with a calm version of her daughter's looks. The brother was younger and was practising to be James Dean. They were waiting to join a party for some outing.

They were affluent with their friendship; trying to discover whether they should worry or not. I told them about the picnic and suggested that Laurie take a shirt in case there were mosquitoes. The father asked us back to the Hilton for dinner; Laurie squashed that one, smiling without innocence.

And then Said arrived, very much still in second gear, beaming and being honoured and shaking hands. Laurie threw him in at the deep end. She told her father what a good salesman he was, and the father perceived right- eousness, and Said was very interested in just what suburb of Los Angeles you could find Connecticut, and the state of the car industry, and the father was delighted to find something at last in Europe that was tangible. It was a bit early in the morning for me.

The brother had arrived with the shirt a long while ago, phrases like 'real estate' and 'interest loans' were creeping in; and by that time her daughter could have walked out of the door with Dracula as far as the mother was concerned. Laurie gave up, and sauntered across the lobby with her shoes hanging from one hand and her sunglasses resting on top of her hair. I attempted extradition. The mother was politely in favour, but the father almost came with us. He said as much; how he'd prefer to go back-packing in the forest rather than sit in another goddamn bus. We left him in front of the hotel. Said leap-frogged off the rev counter and screeched us out of the car park, waving zealously.

We all lit cigarettes. There was nothing else to do with jumpy hands. Said had the radio on full-blast and was talking ten to the dozen, full of praise for Americans as though he had suddenly found proof for a personal theory. We stormed out of Florence on the strength of his own private vendetta with Ben Hur; and then Laurie leant forward and switched off the radio.

'If you don't drive slower, Said, I'm going to be sick.'

Carol agreed. 'Just calm down.'

'Where are we going?' I asked.

'We get out of the goddamn city,' Said declared.

Laurie lay across the seat and went to sleep with her head on my lap. Carol taught Said how to use the gears. They relaxed with one another and no word came from the back seats to disturb them. Said became a more cautious driver; Carol laughed at him and he felt able to laugh at himself. The show was over. Carol wasn't at all the pampered dependent that Said wished her to be in his more insecure moments.

We stopped for petrol and she took charge of getting the car filled up; she kept their money in her purse. Said never liked money and hated carrying it around with

151

him. She had some delay with the station attendant; he was quickly out of the car to help her. They walked back arm-in-arm. He kissed her affectionately and she played embarrassed, though she was happy.

As we pulled off the main road and started climbing into the hills, he listened carefully to her instructions about the gears and the danger of breaking an axle or a wheel bearing on the rough country surfaces. She was tactful. She didn't overdo it; careful not to make him feel like a student or a child.

The whole weekend, they never once talked to each other about the market or her travels except when Said, on the drive back, suddenly gripped the wheel and muttered something about eight more weeks. Then she lit him a cigarette and rested her head on his shoulder.

We went through San Donato, the people watched us from their café with expressionless peasant interest, and we drove on. The road stopped climbing and we could have taken any of the tracks that led off into the forest. Said chose one at random. He got very worried as the car lurched in and out of the pot-holes. He decided that we should stop. Laurie was coming out of her doze and Carol sat on the car seat with the door open, looking at the silence. Said prowled around, marking out the territory, badly wanting to do something.

'We eat,' he announced, heading for the back of the car.

'Not yet; let Laurie sleep, poor girl.' Carol closed the car door behind her. 'Let's go up the track.'

'I drive. I must learn with the gears.' Said was convinced that Americans never walked anywhere.

'We're not going far . . . ' Carol called to him, already some thirty yards away and holding out a hand.

'Have you got cigarettes, *fiammiferi*?' Said worried.

'Yes.'

'O.K., I come. You come, Robert?'

152

'I'll wait for Laurie,' I said.

'O.K., Carol want to walk. Crazy girl.' He shook his head and put on a cool act to catch up with her. He didn't like being watched from behind. He seemed to ask her again about the car and she laughed at him. He gesticulated helplessly. They set off in earnest.

They wouldn't get far. He hung on her shoulder and looked incongruous in his tight trousers and high-heeled shoes. They made it round the bend with two stops to examine the shoes for damage.

I put Laurie's head on a cushion and eased myself as gently as I could out of the car. The heat inside was too stifling for a job as a motionless head-rest. I strolled back the way we had come and found a clump of rock off to the right from where I could see down to the village and across to the layered terraces which the peasants farmed.

There wasn't even a dog barking. The noon kept everything quiet, everything that didn't want to be grilled. Up here there was a breeze which took the edge off the heat, leaving the scenery idle and placid.

'Robert . . . '

Laurie was close, but I was invisible from the road.

'Robert?'

'Over here.'

She arrived with some cushions, flushed with car-sleep.

'This is fine.'

'I was just going to wake you.'

She looked around her for a moment, acknowledging the homage of nature. She arranged the cushions and took off her jeans and bikini, lying under the cover of her sunglasses.

Down in the village, the men were all sitting outside the café in their Sunday suits and the old women were smothered in black, across the square in the shade of the trees.

It was difficult to ignore the naked body, not to flick bits of stone at it or to caress it. It was like a smooth, humid patch of clay on a baked ground; anyone human would have wanted to leave their impression, a child would have pushed her finger into it, an old man would have poked with his stick into its softness. She wore her nakedness like most Europeans wore clothes; stylishly.

She held out a cushion. I took it and walked past her, sitting down at her feet. She drew up her knees and I leaned back on them. This was some sort of treaty, amiable and respectful. The hills and the valley had a sensuality which she was carefree enough not to challenge.

The rock left white scratches on her skin, and the sun brought sweat out between her breasts and around her hairlines. She was as motionless and as spread as the terraces on the opposite hill, with the moisture being drawn out of them, with tentative smells and unconscious movements below the skin. We lay there for a long time.

There was a sudden burst of the loud and grotesque music that surrounds beauty in Italy, which reminds the foreigner that not everything can be culturally static. In this case, it came from the car radio.

'Looks like Said's back.' Laurie didn't move. 'They should come up here, it's a good place to eat.'

'There won't be anywhere better. I'll get them.' I stood up, and looked at the beautiful skin.

'How do you feel about clothes?' I hinted.

'Against. Hell, he must have seen naked women before. I'm not giving anyone the come-on.'

'I wouldn't say that. You're not the ugliest naked girl I've ever seen.'

'Why, thank you.' She shifted languorously.

'You can never tell what you might do to people without meaning to.'

'Do you think it will be a hassle?'

'I don't know. Do what you like. There'll be a hell of a

154

hassle if we don't get to make love tonight.'

'There won't be any hassle about that . . . ' She took off her sunglasses and rubbed her side. 'Let's sneak away.'

'Let's wait.'

'I want to sneak off and make love. I don't care. I don't care if we never go back.' She stretched her arms over her head and posed the question.

It was difficult.

'Got to be polite, I suppose. Good manners.' She changed over on to her front and re-arranged her abandon.

'Shame,' I commiserated.

The smile spread across her cheek.

'In the States you never have to wait for anything; that's what I like about it.'

'I'll go down to the village and start forming a queue.'

She lazily threw a stone after me.

Said was hot and bothered when I arrived at the car, and Carol was amused. He never perspired in the cauldron of the market place, but without anything to do he was bothered; and he wasn't a mute admirer of the countryside. Carol sent him on ahead with a couple of inflatable mattresses, while she and I sorted out the provisions. I told him to call out to Laurie.

'We didn't bring anything.' I stated the obvious.

'That's all right; in between midnight and waking up in the car, I didn't think you'd have time to buy much. Is Laurie hungry?' Carol had a pile of cheese and mortadella and fruit, and a large bottle of white wine.

'Laurie's flat out in the sun. She got tired of clothes.'

'Oh, Said won't know where to put himself,' Carol laughed.

'We thought of that; she decided to roll over on to her stomach.'

'Oh well, if you've got it you should show it; that's American. I'd guess that she's got it, she's a looker. Good

155

on her.' She closed the boot of the car.

'You've got nothing to complain about.'

She looked at me, smiling with her mouth turned down.

'I don't have to give it away, honey. I hope it didn't sound like I was jealous. The bitch.' We laughed, and walked slowly down the track. 'She's young and having a ball. She's going Monday; you know?'

'I don't think I'll die of a broken heart.'

'I just thought I'd tell you. Just in case.'

We had slowed almost to a halt.

'Are you going to go?' I asked her.

'Where to?' She wasn't anxious to answer.

'Back to the States.'

'Why?'

'It must be difficult. I'm nosey. Is it?'

'I'm not in it just to get laid, if that's what you mean. At my age you get a bit depressed in the morning. I was married and divorced in California. I worked hard and saved to come over to Europe. So there's going back to California and there's Said. Do I stay here alone or do I stay here with him? Do I go back with him or do I go back alone? We don't think about it. I guess that's wrong. We need sorting out. Maybe it's best to let the Government decide. If that doesn't sound too cold. He's a great guy, isn't he?'

'Yes, he . . . '

'He's in it just the same; he doesn't know what to do. He's happy when he's talking a lot of bull about California. He protects me more from California than he does from Europe and you can imagine how he is on protection. I have to take the car and get away from him. Period. He can be too much. But I guess that having him there stops me getting picked off by someone a lot worse than him. Don't let anyone kid you, there are plenty of sharks in Europe; you can get cleaned out on a fast romance. Americans are very simple when it comes to playing lovers. You feel naked in Europe until you learn to be suspicious. I've been lucky.'

'He feels the same way.'

'That English charm; I don't know . . . ' She laughed, but was shy.

'It's natural,' I joked.

'Like hell it is. You've got Laurie lying out there naked.'

'You're not kidding me that she doesn't know what she's after?'

'It isn't hard to figure out. Two days doesn't leave you much time to get involved. And you needn't think that I'm dead. Just a bit older and a bit more serious. And a lot less American. More aware. And responsible; you needn't worry about that. It's not as though I've got any home to feel homesick about. I'll keep my clothes on.' We started walking again. Carol brushed aside her worry. 'I can't afford to give her the pleasure. Or maybe I don't care to.'

We turned off the track and began the short climb. She slowed. Her confidence disappeared suddenly.

'I don't know what I am now. That's not very American, is it? Maybe I should go back, before it's too late. Do they love in Europe?'

'Why not?' I took the wine from her.

'You're too young to get nervous about it. We'd better give Said the sunglasses so that he can look at her without being noticed.' She smiled across the rocks.

Said was frantic with occupation while Laurie sprawled supine in front of him. I'd seen it before. Carol was interested, but Said was having a hard time.

'Am I flipping anyone out?' Laurie murmured.

'No, honey; you just stay right where you are. Said's quite used to statues and he's just wondering what price he could get for you. I think you're just beautiful. It's always better to get a tan all over if you can, otherwise the whole trip wouldn't be worthwhile.'

Laurie eyed Carol warily, but couldn't make her out. She said it was hot and went back to lying on her stomach. Said was still unsure how to react. Carol put down the food and watched him.

'We forgot the bread, Robert.'

'I get it.' Said was keen to be away. 'I am going, Robert. We have cigarettes?'

'Yes, we're fine; just the bread.'

'O.K.' Said scrambled off the rock and disappeared.

'It's so hot,' Laurie groaned, 'I think I'm burning up.'

'Sometimes with the wind you don't realise it. I got burned just yesterday. I can't take too much sun.' Carol sat on a mattress and started to spread out the food.

'Maybe you're right. I guess I'm just dumb that way. I'll get into my jeans and a shirt.'

'Let me put a little oil on your shoulders.'

There was no loss of face; the way they arranged it between them. Laurie turned her back modestly, and Carol kept her eyes on the food. I rubbed the oil lightly over Laurie's skin before she buttoned up. Said appeared not to notice any difference when he came back.

There was an atmosphere of exhilarated release, which tempted everybody. We drank a lot and snacked the food. We started a cabaret where Carol and Laurie played the range of stereotyped tourists to our feverish salesmen and thwarted seducers. It left them helpless with laughter as they ridiculed and baited us. They were very tight as a team.

Then, just as suddenly, the mood snapped as Carol poked Said with a burst of uncontrollable mockery. Said raged in Italian and stamped off down the path. Carol smiled nervously. She excused herself and went after him.

Laurie and I were too crazy to care. We were far too amorous to brood over the temper that was scudding across the afternoon. We lay along the airbed, provoking

158

and giggling, half serious, half careless.

'Oh shit . . . '

'Not again . . . '

The car had started revving up.

And then we were both in as bad a temper as he was, slumping deprived into the back seat, everything pivoting wildly around the sudden change in the driver. Like a compass needle gone mad, we hurtled back down the hillside in silence with the food skating from side to side along the shelf under the back window. Said was stolen by his fury. We were too cautious and resentful to say anything about it. But he would have to be restored; before we got killed.

'Don't get screwed up, Said. You'll make a million dollars anywhere,' Laurie lured him.

'Perhaps.' Said kept his eyes fixed on the road. 'You think so?' The speed dropped slightly.

'Sure,' Laurie went on. 'You're an honest guy; you come over straight when you're selling.'

'You listen?' Said told Carol.

'I know that, honey. We were only fooling around up there.' She reached uncertainly for his arm but he didn't give her any encouragement; her hand stayed forlornly on his shoulder.

'You know how good you are with the women; you could sell a woman anything. And in the States it's always the women that count, you know? My mother can get anything from my father.'

'I sell her a statue; I think she remember me this morning when we were in the hotel.' Said nodded.

'Sure you did. You could have sold her anything.'

'Is true. Any American woman, I sell.'

'Not every American woman,' Carol squeezed his shoulder.

'Not Carol. You know, Robert, I never sell anything to Carol in the market. She is different. Then I like her for the first time. I tell her I try again tomorrow. She comes along and we fall in love.'

He kissed the hand that gave him a cigarette.

'I bet I could sell her a string of onions,' I claimed. Said choked with laughter and dismissed me out of hand. 'With Carol? Never. You think she is stupid? My friend, this woman is intelligent. She know about painting. She know everything about me. What for she need Giorgio's onions; maybe a beautiful statue, only six of them in the world, very cheap, ten thousand lire . . . '

'I'll buy it,' Carol ruffled his hair, 'but only because of the salesman.'

'I steal it for you, my lover.' There was a sustained burst of applause from the back seats. Laurie and I withdrew back into each other. Said concentrated on the finer points of driving. He wanted to put an arm round Carol, but he didn't trust himself with the car.

'You want me to drive?' Carol suggested.

'I think so.'

He pulled into the side of the road and they changed seats. Then he could put his arm round her.

'It's early, isn't it?' Laurie asked.

'It's a quarter of five.' Carol drove slowly.

'Can we stop off somewhere, out of the city?'

'Let's stop off at the Belvedere.' I liked the Belvedere.

'Where's that?' Laurie mumbled from a drowse.

'It's a good place to watch the sun go down,' I told her.

'Is very beautiful.' Said classified it.

We talked about beauty on the way down, mainly Carol and I, about Fiesole and even the fish market in Venice. Laurie was arranged into her own coyness and Said might have replied that he was thinking of Jordan if anyone had asked him. It whiled away the journey.

We parked on the Piazzale Michelangiolo and strolled along the wall. I pointed out the city to Laurie, the orange urn of the *duomo* and the towers of the palaces.

'It's beautiful. And I am drunk; but it's all beautiful . . . '
She looked at me unsteadily.

'Are you very drunk?' I wondered.

'I don't know. Just emotional . . . ' She gave a wide
sweep with her arm, round and over the city roofs and
back around me, hugging up to my ear. 'It's all a bit too
much . . . ' she whispered.

We lay out on the terraced grass under the Fortress,
side by side, keeping an eye on the sky as the sun fell
behind the hills. The noise of the traffic trickled down the
slopes into the bowl of buildings. Said held Carol's hand
and smoked cigarettes; he was miles away. The girls lay
on their backs, hiding themselves behind their sunglasses, letting the effects of the wine wear off.

Carol murmured something to Said.

'Yes, I go now,' Said got quickly to his feet and brushed
the grass off his trousers. 'You are thirsty, Laurie?'

'I guess so.' Laurie ran her tongue over her lips.

'I am going to fetch some water. You will wait here,
Robert?'

'We're not going anywhere. Do you want company?'

'Again?'

'Do you want anyone to go with you, darling?' Carol
asked.

'No. It is not good for driving fast. I see you, ten,
maybe fifteen minutes. O.K.?' We nodded our gratitude
and watched him walk across the grass and off along the
wall.

'He's such a nice guy,' Laurie thought aloud. We heard
the car start.

'I don't know if I owe you an apology for what
happened back there . . . ' Carol hesitated.

'Don't be stupid,' I said.

'Hell, no, it was just weird', Laurie's voice probed. 'If
you can't be weird once in a while, who wants to go on
living?'

There was a pause while Carol considered whether to allow her any closer. She was very unsure. She knew that Laurie was waiting; she didn't know if Laurie was old enough to have any sympathy. Laurie lay passively.

'He doesn't like to see me drink any alcohol.'

Laurie caught Carol's smile and rallied to her.

'Well, that's tough! What about smoking grass?'

'We never have.'

'Carol, what d'you *do* the whole time?' Laurie propped herself up on one elbow; so sympathetic, so concerned, so serious.

'We seem to get along.'

I moved away from them to sit on a wall and look out over the late afternoon. Their conversation progressed into intimacy. The words came and swished away from me like a restless chiffon of gnats.

'It looks like you're in love.'

'I feel that way.'

'What are they going to think back home?'

'Oh they gave up on me a long time ago. I was divorced already. My mother thought it was such a good idea that she did it too. She nearly came over here with me . . . '

'That would be terrible.' They laughed.

'You said it.'

'I know it. You should see my mother in Europe . . . '

I reflected that there was nothing wrong with Laurie's mother in Europe that the absence of her father wouldn't cure. I wondered why Said didn't aim at that age bracket. He would have made a lot more money escorting well-preserved mothers on their second phase of youth, and somewhere along the line one of them would have got him some papers in return for forgetting about her. I shook my head sadly; this was Sunday, the market didn't start until tomorrow.

'You just didn't get along?'

'You could say that. He liked to drink beer and watch

the ball game on television. I wanted to get educated. It was a good decision.'

'You think you'll go back home again in the Fall?'

'Maybe. This is like home for me now.'

'Yeah, I can see that . . .' Laurie wasn't convinced, and the doubt hovered. Carol made a half-hearted attempt to flap it away.

'You must come from a place much prettier than Redondo Beach, Los Angeles.'

'Connecticut? It's pretty . . .'

No. Said wouldn't make a million in Connecticut. Maybe in New Jersey. But making a million in New Jersey would destroy him. Much better California and the medical insurance and the tiny swimming pool pushed up against the barbecue patio. Surely she would protect him from it all – or would she start buying paper plates. Cars with automatic gears weren't *that* expensive in Europe.

'I'll write you.'

'I don't have an address in L.A. any more.'

'Well when you and Said get over there . . . it won't take them long to fix the papers, will it? And we might be flying out to California in the Christmas vacation. I could come and look you up . . .' Laurie persisted.

'Maybe . . . maybe . . . why don't you take our address in Florence? If we go back to the States, I'll write you.'

'That's fine. You think you'll stick with Said?' Laurie threw it away so carelessly. Carol reached for another cigarette.

'You must get sick of it . . .' I interrupted from the wall.

'This is an American conversation, between two American girls, if you can keep your butt where it is . . .' Laurie slammed back. 'She could tell me to mind my own business, thank you. We don't all need treating like we were some kind of stupid kids playing around in front of good old father, we get sick of being told what a dumb

163

country we come from. We're not dead yet, man; we look at things as we see them. If you want to look away, you go right ahead and steam up. There's too much crap around.'

Carol smiled back over her shoulder.

'It *is* bullshit; that's true, isn't it?' Laurie pleaded. 'Or should I keep my mouth shut . . . '

'No . . . ' Carol and I both said it. Laurie flung herself back on the grass.

'Sometimes I get so paranoid in this country; whatever it is.'

'So do I . . . ' Carol put her arm round Laurie's neck. 'It comes through to you.'

'You think that's what it is? I suppose it's lucky I'm running for home, dammit. Dammit.' She clenched her fist and pounded it on the grass. I sat beside her.

'At least you know what to expect if you come back again.'

'I've had a good time here. When Said comes we'll all sit in a circle and hug and I'll say thank you.' She sat up and hung on, to hide away from eyes. Carol crept close. I could see her trying to stop thinking. There was a car racing up the hill, a second gear straining above the noise of the traffic.

'I'll go and tell him where we're at.' Carol extricated herself.

Laurie didn't move; she hung on to the comfort.

'Too much wine . . . ' she whispered.

'Don't worry,' I told her, 'you don't have to cover yourself.'

'I've had such a good time, Robert. With you and Carol and Said. I was going back to the States all screwed up. Really tight. It would have been terrible. Even my father was worried, I know he was. He made me come. I had this boyfriend, we were going to spend the summer at the Cape . . . it's been so good.'

164

'You've only got Spain, then you'll be back,' I commiserated.

'I don't care about him. He was a real nothing; zilch . . . shall we write . . . ?'

'O.K.'

The city was over her shoulder, and the grass was getting damp as the sun left it.

'You must know Europe pretty good . . . ' she asked quietly.

'I don't know Spain or Norway, and I don't know anything about Eastern Europe,' I considered; 'otherwise I've been to a few places.'

'We don't want to visit Eastern Europe,' she murmured.

'No.'

The sun sharpened the outline of the hills and the roofs died away like embers, as they did almost every evening, from red through to the grey, ashen colour of the dawn mist which floated on the Arno. No one had yet got round to producing a postcard of that moment, but they would.

'It gets cold.'

Laurie and I looked up at Said. He had one arm round Carol and the other holding a couple of sweaters from the car.

'You can say that again.' Laurie clambered into the wool. We had our drink and we had a hug for a minute or two, Said clinging on to Carol, his eyes escaping to survey us.

'You not go tomorrow,' he shook his head at Laurie, 'you stay here with Robert and we get a big house together.'

'Said . . . ' Carol tweaked his arm.

'Why not? I don't understand why she must go; why do you go? Why always going? What for?'

'It sounds like a great idea. I want to stay, Said, but it's all arranged.' Laurie nodded in shame.

'Why is it all arranged? How can this be?'
'Because it is and it is. I'll come back; honestly I will.'
Laurie drew into me protectively.
'Stupid women,' Said beamed.
'Stop giving everyone a hard time.' Carol nudged him
sternly, smiling across at us.
'I give her a hard time? Who is? Why I am doing this?'
He was horrified.
'No, no . . .' Laurie put out a hand.
'You see . . .' he glared at Carol.
'We interrupted them, honey,' she explained, a little
uncertain whether it was all getting out of control again.
'Yes, I see this. We go. We wait for you at the car.' He
whirled Carol around at the end of his arm and they
started back.
'Hang on . . .' Laurie and I ran after them and
engulfed them into a line of four, laughing across the
dusk. Said played innocent.
'Sometimes,' he shouted, 'it is impossible to understand.'
'Give up,' I suggested.
'Give up, give up, Said, that's what you gotta do!'
Laurie squeezed him breathless on top of the Fort. He
tried to arrange his dignity and gave up with good grace.
It was the only time I saw him look less than confident.
He asked me on the Wednesday whether I thought Los
Angeles was full of women like Laurie. He seemed to
regard her departure as something of a mixed blessing
for me. It was, perhaps, not good to have such a
demanding girl always close to you. For making love
sometimes it was good, but for sharing an apartment it
was too annoying, too much noise; and the word
'presence' was what he was looking for as he flicked
anxiously through the slim dictionary in his mind. He
always remained sceptical of Laurie; even when I joked
about her, he shook his head as if to try to get her into
perspective. She gave him an uneasy feeling about

America. It drew him closer to Carol for the time that they had left.

We walked over the gravel at the top of the Belvedere and shied clear of the bevy of late sightseers who were gazing up at the David. There was an evening service at the San Miniato church, lights and the sound of a choir echoing through the trees.

'Have you ever been there?' Carol asked Laurie.

'I don't think I have.' She had no idea.

'Is beautiful,' Said allotted.

'It's tiny, and it's nice inside.' Carol was insistent.

'I'd like to see it.'

'We'll go across there right now.'

Said's shoulders slumped visibly in the gloom. Carol and Laurie set the pace. Said and I ambled in their slipstream. There was nothing to talk about except the market; Said peered at his watch.

'It can't be more than seven-thirty,' I reckoned.

'Eight,' he contradicted, 'and now we have to go to a church.'

'It'll do us good. For the soul.'

'You think so?'

'No.'

'I don't think so, Robert. All the church make too much money selling shit. I tell you, you think the market is good; and the Church is much more money than the market. I have always tell this to Giulio but he is an idiot bastard. Someday I will get a black dress like they have and stand in the high seat and tell all the people they are bad sinning and they must buy a lot of shit or they will die horrible with a knife in hell. Is easy to sell if you talk like that. Is easy for the stupid people to believe. Giulio, he does not even sell the crucifix in the market. He is afraid of the Church. He think they bring five, ten men and break the market. I say we get ten, twenty men, friends, and fight them. Then we sell their shit on the market and

167

make a lot of money. But Giulio, hah, I tell you . . . ' Said spread his mouth distastefully, 'Giulio has the heart of a pig. He is afraid even of his wife . . . '

It was presumably the hour of the day when Said prepared himself for the ritual Monday struggle. He reeled off a list of insults and curses, exorcising himself in a long and increasingly boring monologue. I grunted in agreement whenever he paused for confirmation, but I didn't give it much thought. It was a replica of the torrent that poured from him whenever he came across the street after being sacked. I vaguely wondered if tomorrow would be one of those days.

I wondered if I could manage to get the sack, but Giorgio was just too easy-going. He needed only an occasional translator, not a salesman. It would be another six days of smiling patiently at dumpy couples and springing the occasional cruel disappointment on English punters who liked wrestling with their mindlocked Italian phrases. It didn't bear thinking about.

Why not talk Laurie into leaving the tour with a few dollars from her father?

But it was arranged. She wouldn't stay on; it would never occur to her. A weekend was our limit. She wouldn't let go of her schedule. Anyone who wanted to stay looked around for something definite to do, some way of getting involved with the city so that its permanence didn't make you feel so insignificant. Better perhaps to be in transit.

We arrived at the door to the church. Said stopped cursing and looked inside, suddenly sheepish for a moment. We couldn't see Laurie or Carol. We waited with a cigarette, feeling like a couple of gigolos.

'I see you at the market.' Said spat.

'Yes, we'll walk home. I expect we'll stop and eat something on the way; if you're interested.'

'We go to the apartment.'

'What's Carol doing this week?'

'I don't know, Robert. Maybe she is going to Austria. Is good for her, she thinks. Intelligent girl and lousy cook. Divorced.'

They came out of the church, whispering and smiling.

'We go now, say goodbye to you and a happy travel.' Said stepped forward.

'We can give them a ride, honey,' Carol frowned.

'I thought we'd walk down the hill and have something to eat on the way. It isn't far. Said's exhausted and he has to be up before I do.'

'So it's goodbye,' Laurie sighed.

'I guess so.' Carol took Said's arm.

'I suppose it sounds dumb, but it was really great meeting with you.' Laurie was humbled nearly into tears.

'You get an address?' Said demanded.

'Sure thing.' Carol tapped her purse.

'We write. Then we come to see you. Maybe your father gives me a job.'

'Oh he will. I'll tell him when I see him tomorrow.'

'We say goodbye not for very long,' Said concluded happily.

'You have a good trip home.'

'I will . . . ' Laurie cried. We walked slowly out along the road. Said and Carol took the opposite direction.

'They're such a neat couple, I'm really going to miss them . . . '

We walked past the Belvedere again and on down a small road which wound into the centre of the city. It was much too steep to carry any sobs.

'It's no use being sad,' Laurie blew her cares away, 'I'll see them again.'

'Of course you will.'

She was light-hearted and bold, crying and laughing at herself, warm salt lips and turbulence. She wanted to be loved.

There wasn't anywhere open to eat, except for the bar downstairs. It was better than the Scotsman, Laurie agreed, but she still had to go up to the flat for a moment to wash her face clear of the day and rub the faintest of lipstick and eyeshadow over the sun. We had toasted sandwiches and *grappa* in the raucous surroundings and she felt more at home amongst the unshaven segment of the city. She won at pinball, much to her prediction.

'I suppose you feel good.'

'I feel good.'

We played another game before leaving the bar. I was winning before she got annoyed and tilted the table.

The alarm clock reached her before it reached me. It was dawn again, but it was Monday. She made no move. I leaned over her and cut it off.

'Come on.' I tapped her shoulder.

'What time do you have to go to the market?' She was alive.

'Another couple of hours.'

'I don't eat breakfast.'

It was ten-thirty when we woke up again, and I was by the window, checking through my pockets for spare change and keys, before she pushed the hair out of her face and pretended to stretch.

'I'm late,' I said, 'I've got to go.'

'We don't get picked up from the hotel until three in the afternoon.'

'I'm working; I must go.'

'Robert, you can take a day off.'

'No.'

'I bet you can.'

I sat by her on the bed for a moment; she was lovely; warm with her own musk.

'Send me a letter.'

'I'm not going.'

170

'O.K., then stay here. I'd like you to. I mean it. I'll see you this evening, or in the market at lunchtime.'

I hugged her and went out of the door. The Scotsman was in the kitchen.

'Good morning,' he said, drily.

'Her name's Laurie.' I drank off a glass of milk and went downstairs, leaving him to worry about how many eggs he should put in the boiling water.

I shook my head clear. I walked quickly down to the river. And then, half-way across the bridge, I thought that it was Monday, and Monday was a quiet day. The tourists all came and went on Monday. They never reached the markets until the afternoon; except for the surreal Japanese. Monday was a busy day for hotel staff; there wasn't much call for salesmen. It was the day for sitting on the steps in the shade and not caring what the browser did with his cash. Who bothered about raffia fruit anyway? It wasn't a religion. I remembered her lying out on the rock in the sun. And tilting the pinball machine.

Said was sitting in the café.

'What's happening?' I moved in opposite him.

'Nothing. Very quiet.' He smoothed down the front of his hair.

'Giorgio all right?'

'Sure. I tell him you are in love. He understands this. I argue with Giulio then I help Giorgio. Now I wait for the pig to buy me a drink.'

'I'm not going to stay around. I'll be in tomorrow. Or I'll be in Spain.'

'Sure.' Said was preoccupied.

'Carol O.K.?'

'Yes. She has gone with the car.'

'I'll see you.'

'No problems with Giorgio. You take three days, three weeks.'

'Good.'

'*Ciao.*'

I went back through the city to my flat, but the Scotsman had got rid of her in his inevitable style. She had left the candle that she had bought from San Miniato, and her address in Connecticut. The Scotsman was typing in his bedroom. I poked my head round the door and glared at him. He looked up, startled.

'Sorry to interrupt you,' I said, 'I just came back to check.'

'There was no suicide note.' He sneaked himself a smile.

His sense of humour was founded on fifteenth-century anecdote and granite. The next time, he could rot in jail. I had to blame somebody. There was no point in going to the hotel.

ABOUT THE AUTHOR

Richard Thornley was born in 1950 in the West Midlands. He has
lived in Cambridge, London, Savoy, New Hampshire, Wiltshire and
New Jersey. He presently lives in the Carmel Valley in California
with his wife and daughter. *Zig-Zag*, his first book, was first
published in London by Jonathan Cape, Ltd. His second book,
Attempts to Join Society was published here in the States in 1986.
Richard Thornley is presently at work on a novel set in the
southwest.